Throwing Knives

Throwing Knives

Winner of the Sandstone Prize in Short Fiction

MOLLY BEST TINSLEY

Ohio State University Press

Columbus

Library of Congress Cataloging-in-Publication Data
Tinsley, Molly Best.
Throwing knives / Molly Best Tinsley.
p.   cm.
"Winner of the Sandstone Prize in Short Fiction."
Contents: Zoe—Square zero—Figure drawing—White—
Affairs of strangers—Holiday—The only way to ride—Throwing knives—
Mother tongue—Outbound—Welcome advance—Everyone catch on love.
ISBN 0-8142-0847-9 (alk. paper)—ISBN 0-8142-5051-3 (pbk.: alk. paper)
1. United States—Social life and customs—20th century—Fiction. I. Title.
PS3570.I57 T48 2000
813'.54—dc21   99-053749

Text and jacket design by Paula Newcomb.
Type set in Galliard by Tseng Information Systems, Inc.
Printed by Thomson-Shore, Inc.

The paper used in this publication meets the minimum
requirements of the American National Standard for
Information Sciences—Permanence of Paper for Printed
Library Materials. ANSI Z39.48-1992.

9 8 7 6 5 4 3 2 1

Acknowledgments

Stories in this collection originally appeared in the following magazines:

"Affairs of Strangers"	*Prairie Schooner*
"Everyone Catch on Love"	*West Branch*
"Holiday"	*Shenandoah*
"Mother Tongue"	*Greensboro Review*
"The Only Way to Ride"	*Prairie Schooner*
"Outbound"	*New England Review/ Bread Loaf Quarterly*
"Square Zero"	*American Letters and Commentary*
"Throwing Knives"	*Redbook*
"Welcome Advance"	*Prairie Schooner*
"White"	*New England Review*
"Zoe"	*Shenandoah.* Reprinted in *Pushcart Prize, XVII*

I am indebted to the National Endowment for the Arts and to the Naval Academy Research Council for the generous grants that gave me the time and encouragement to create.

For Ed

Contents

Zoe

SHE tried to be the first to speak. It wasn't that she wanted to be nice, put them at ease; it was her way of warning them not to be, of setting the tone she did best: bemused, even ironic, but formal. She never wanted any of them thinking she was someone to cultivate. Whenever those voices, low and strained, interrupted her life downstairs, whether they came late at night from the front hall or mornings from the kitchen, she'd slip into the one-piece camouflage suit she used as a bathrobe, wrap the belt twice around her slim waist, and ascend to meet her mother's latest. She liked to catch him with breakfast in his mouth, or romance on his mind, and then before he could compose himself, announce, "I am Zoe, her daughter," offering a little bow and a graceful hand, limp as japonica.

It usually left him stammering, fumbling—this blend of child-like respect and self-possession. If he'd already begun to imagine her mother recharging his life with pleasure and purpose, Zoe's winsome presence could make such visions more intense, then tip them into unsettling. Though he'd never gone in for kids before, he found himself thinking at first how agreeable it would be to have a delicate creature like her around, slender, long-legged, with pale freckles across her nose and auburn hair. These days she has it bobbed at the ears, curling up shorter in back above a softly fringed nape. But if he thought for a moment how much the child must know, her poise could seem ominous—all the things *he* didn't know, hungered to find out, might not want to hear.

"So what's it like, living with her?" one of them asked Zoe once, as if he expected soon to be sharing the experience. He reminded Zoe of a large rabbit—a confusion of timidity and helpless lust.

"There's never a dull moment," Zoe answered, sweet but nonchalant. "I meet a lot of interesting men." That was stretching things. Most have been rabbits.

Often they felt called upon to tell Zoe, "Your mom's a great lady." Did they think Zoe was responsible for raising her mother and not the other way around? Or that she had a choice of mothers? Or that she couldn't guess what they really meant, that her mother was something else in bed, that they'd never done it to a Sibelius symphony before?

Since the age of five, when her parents split up, Zoe Cameron and her mother, Phyllis Rush, have lived beyond the D.C. Beltway in the Colonies of Virginia, clusters of townhouses subtly tucked into one hundred acres of rolling woods, whose inhabitants have readily paid a little more to get aesthetic design and proximity to nature. Set into the ridge of a hill, with high ceilings and an expanse of glass to the south, Zoe's mother's unit welcomes light, draws it in to challenge her work—heavy terra-cotta, here and there a dull giant bronze—set off by white walls. Each piece has been given a woman's name, yet they are only parts of women, global buttocks and thighs, pairs of breasts larger than the heads mounted upon them—Leda, Electra, Helen, truncated. They are one reason Zoe has stopped bringing home friends, who tend to stare in stunned silence or whisper words like *gross* and *perverted*. Zoe has learned contempt for kids her own age, who cannot understand true art.

Yet she hates her mother's women: fat, naked blobs. The bald definition of nipple or vulva makes her sick.

There are more of them on exhibit in the local gallery her mother manages in the Commons. The public tends not to buy them, but Phyllis does enter them in shows and they have won awards, including a purchase prize at the Corcoran. After that a man from *The Washington Post* came out to photograph Phyllis at home in her skylit studio. Zoe declined to be in any of his shots. He took her mother to dinner in Great Falls. When Zoe came up the next morning to leave for school, he was in the kitchen alone, making raisin toast. He offered her a slice, trying to act as if he owned the place, but she drank her sixteen ounces of water as if he weren't there. It was easier than ever to resist that sweet yeasty aroma, tainted as it was by his male pride.

BUT this Lucas—nothing has been easy about him. If only she could go back and start over again with the moment she arrived home in the early afternoon to find his body sticking out from under the sink. Thinking her mother had finally called someone to fix the dishwasher, Zoe set her wide-brimmed hat down on the table and looked on absently as the body twisted and grunted with its efforts. Her hunger had been stubborn that day, conjuring extravagant food fantasies that almost sabotaged a test in precalculus. But she had conquered temptation, and now what she wanted was plenty of water and maybe a carrot to get through until dinner.

"Lemme out of here," came a roar, all of a sudden, followed by bumping sounds and *great god*'s, and the upper part of the man extricated itself from the cabinet. His knuckles were smudged with black, his once-starched shirt was sharply wrinkled, and he rubbed the top of his head ruefully, but when he saw Zoe, his expression flexed in a smile. "Well, look at you," he said. "Aren't you just dressed to kill!"

And not expecting such a remark from a repairman, Zoe, who was known to become transfixed by her own image wherever she found it reflected, who that day was wearing one of her favorite suits—broadly padded shoulders over a short slim skirt, a blue that turned her eyes blue—could not bring herself to disagree, nor think of anything to say back. She did try her ironic geisha bow, but in the same instant noticed the roaches hurrying over the sill of the sink cabinet and out across the kitchen floor in a dark stream.

Before she knew it she had emitted a soft scream, more out of embarrassment than fear. She had certainly seen roaches in the kitchen before, those nights when she gave in to temptation and felt her way up the stairs in the dark, thinking it was almost like sleepwalking, she was almost not responsible for what she was about to do, forage for food, cookies, bagels, leftover pasta, cinnamon raisin toast drenched in butter. When she turned on the light, there they always were, collected on some vertical surface in clusters of imperceptible activity, and she caught her breath in disgust, but went on to get what she had come for.

"They must have a nest under there," the man said, a little out of breath. He was somehow hopping and stooping at the same time, slapping at the creatures with one of his moccasins. "How about giving me a hand here?"

Zoe looked down helplessly at her clothes, her inch-high patent heels.

"How about insecticide, a spray or something?"

"If we have any, it's in there." She pointed to the cabinet from which they kept coming. The floor around him was awash with brown spots. Some had been hit and were finished moving. "Close the door," Zoe cried. When she realized the sense of her suggestion, she repeated it more calmly.

He smacked the door shut, and the stream was cut off. "Good thinking," he said.

She pursed her lips to hide her pleasure. Producing a fly swatter from the closet in the front hall, she commenced ceremoniously to slap at the remaining roaches from the comfortable distance its handle allowed. "Mother," she called.

"She went to the store," the man said, rubbing his bare foot along his pants leg then replacing his shoe. "I thought I'd keep myself busy until she got back."

That was when Zoe realized he wasn't a plumber and that she

had been inexplicably foolish. Her mother, who scorned home maintenance, who refused to spend any time on fixing things, when she could be making something new—why would her mother suddenly hire a plumber? "I am Zoe, her daughter," she said, with a final stroke of the swatter, but it was too late.

"I assumed as much," the man said. "From the side you're a dead ringer." He introduced himself: Lucas Washburn. He had light almost frizzy hair and eyebrows, no cheekbones to speak of, and his nose must have been broken once and never set straight. His skin was fissured from past acne, and his eyes were a flat, changeless gray. He was not handsome, Zoe decided, but there was something about him. His hair was cropped short, his skin evenly tanned, his khaki pants creased. Clean—in spite of his disarray, he seemed oddly, utterly clean.

"I assumed you were the plumber." Zoe pulled the broom out from beside the refrigerator and began with dignity to sweep roach hulls into a pile.

"I can see why. I hear you're down to one bathtub."

Zoe stiffened at the forced intimacy, the hint of sympathy. She normally did not interfere in her mother's affairs, patiently allowing what Phyllis would call nature to take its course. But this man, with his long cheekless face, who had poked around under their sink, discovered their roaches—he was not at all her mother's type, and the sooner he was history, the better. She said, "Well, it happens to be my bathtub downstairs, which gets pretty inconvenient. One of my mom's quote friends end quote pulled the soap holder off the wall in *her* tub and half the tiles came with it, and the guest tub has a leak that drips into the front hall. Actually, the whole house is a total wreck." She finished, and made herself laugh, but in the silence that was his reply, she heard her words echo like a blurted confession, false notes, as if something were playing in the background in a different key. Blasé wasn't working.

"If I had my tools," Lucas said, "we could get this sink to drain, and I could take a look at those tubs. Next time I'll bring my tools."

That is a lot to assume, next time, Zoe thought, and to her surprise, that was what she said.

Lucas nodded solemnly then turned his back on her and began washing his hands. Should she explain that her mother had very liberal views, such as, if men and women were allowed to live naturally, without the inhibitions imposed by society, they would choose to spend their nights in each other's beds all the time, different other's beds as the impulse moved them, mornings parting, more often that not, forever? And that was all right with her, Zoe, for it was much worse when a man of her mother's showed up a second time, all twitchy and trembly, and suggested doing something that included her, and her mother, seduced by some transient vision of family, agreed. "I appreciate the warning," Lucas said, drying his long hands finger by finger. Then he added, "But maybe I've got something in common with those guys in there"— he jerked his head toward the roach settlement—"I'm pretty hard to get rid of."

THAT night her mother and Lucas fixed strip steaks, steamed artichokes, wild rice. As she often did, Phyllis set up small folding tables on the balcony off the living room in view of the sunset, but Lucas moved the hibachi to the backyard below to comply with the county fire code. ("What fire code?" Phyllis asked. She had never heard of any fire code.) Zoe went downstairs to change into a faded denim jumpsuit, espadrilles. She rolled a fuchsia bandana into a headband and tied her curls down, Indian-style. She freshened the strip of pale blue shadow on her lower lids. All the while aware that Lucas was right beyond the glass door, the drapes that don't quite meet, calling arguments up to her mother in favor of well-done. Phyllis stuck to rare. Her face blank and impersonal, Zoe made a last appraisal in the full-length mirror. She pushed a fist into her sucked-in abdomen. *I hate my stomach,* she thought. You couldn't trust mirrors; they could be designed to make people look thinner; all the ones in stores tricked you that way.

Lucas sawed off huge blocks of meat and swallowed them almost whole. Her mother plucked her artichoke, petal by petal, dragged each one through her lips slowly, her subtly silvered eyelids drooping with the pleasure. She had a strong jaw, and a wide mouth with large teeth—but she knew how to recontour her face with light and shade, to make her eyes seem bigger, mysterious. Yes, Zoe had her nose, rising fine and straight from the brow, nostrils flared back, so that if you happened to have a cold or be cold, their moisture was open to view. Zoe had learned to carry her head tilted slightly forward, to make it hard for anyone to see into her nose.

To Lucas's credit he seemed not to be noticing Phyllis's sensual performance. He was expressing his suspicion that her clogged dishwasher and drain stemmed from a failure to scrape dirty dishes thoroughly; a small chicken bone in the trap, for example, was all it took to start an obstruction.

Phyllis threw her head back and laughed. "You sound like my mother," she said.

Lucas wasn't fazed. "You're talking to someone who's trained to eliminate human error." Lucas flew for United; Phyllis had picked him out of the happy-hour crowd in the lounge at Dulles Airport after dropping off a friend.

Phyllis stroked his closest arm. "That's mother all over again."

"Another word for it is *accident*."

"It's only a dishwasher," Phyllis said, sullenly, and the fatalist in Zoe settled back with the vaguest sense of loss to watch this man ruin things with her mother long before he could get the bathtubs fixed.

In a steady, almost uninflected voice, he was talking improvements. He could see a brick patio in their backyard, and redwood planters and a hexagonal redwood picnic table. Zoe saw clumsy strategy, tinged with pathos. He frankly admitted he was tired of living on the tenth floor of a condo in River Towers. Between his job and the apartments he unpacked in, he never had his feet on the ground. "It's about time I got my feet on the ground," he said.

"You could sprinkle dirt in your socks," Phyllis said.

She was being strangely tolerant; maybe he had touched off an attack of what she called her *passion for reality*, when practical dailiness, what everyone else did, became the exotic object of curiosity and desire. Lucas was neither suave nor witty. If you sanded his face, he might be handsome. Zoe guessed he had what her mother would call a good body, though she, Zoe, had trouble looking at a male body long enough to form a complete picture of one. She tended to focus on them piece by piece, and they stayed like that in her mind, a jumble of parts. Her mother often said it was an insult to women the way men let themselves go after a certain age, after they had good incomes. Phyllis herself kept her weight down by smoking and thought women should band together and hold men to the same physical standards everyone held women to.

"Why me?" Phyllis asked Lucas, and seemed genuinely to wonder. "For how many years you've been tied to no place particular and been perfectly happy? Why pick on my place? Maybe I like it this way."

"Look at that," Lucas said, pointing above them at a strip of white streaks and blotches on the cedar stain. "Look at the mess those birds have made of your siding. Starlings. They must have a roost in the eaves. I'd have to take care of that before I'd put in a patio right under their flight lines!"

Phyllis pulled forward a lock of her thick dark hair. "I don't begrudge them that. It's nature." She gave a quick yank then let the breeze lift an offending gray strand from her fingers.

"Like roaches under the sink."

Zoe held her breath as her mother lit a cigarette. Was he joking or criticizing? Either way he had no right; either way her mother would finally put him in his place. Then why was she stretching, smiling languidly at his rudeness? "Everyone has them," she said, blowing a plume of smoke. "They're a fact of life."

"You don't have to give in totally," Lucas persisted.

"It isn't in me to go around poisoning things."

Her mother's reasonableness was a puzzle to Zoe. *Why him?* she kept asking herself, until the answer came to her, all at once, made her a little queasy. It was obviously something to do with sex that gave Lucas this power, this license. Wasn't her mother always declaring that everything came down to that? It must be something sexual he did to her mother or for her, which she, Zoe, for all her determined precocity, had not yet figured out. Then she felt very empty—empty as though she had failed an exam; empty because she didn't want to think of Lucas that way. In the back of her mind, she had been hoping he was different, and she didn't even know she was hoping until he turned out to be the same—just another male, who in the irresistible flux of life must soon disappear. Well, she couldn't care less.

THAT night Zoe ate. Once dead silence told her Lucas and her mother had settled down, she stole upstairs in the dark, removed from the freezer a half gallon of vanilla ice cream and went back down to her room. She sat on the bed, and gazing at the photos of lithe models she had cut from her magazines, began to spoon ice cream into her mouth. Each mouthful hit her empty stomach like a cold stone. It made her feel a little crazy, she couldn't think straight anymore. She swung between defiance, when she agreed with herself that this was perfect pleasure, no matter how high the price, this cool, bland sweetness, this private solitude—defiance—and despair. "Eat up," she heard her mother encouraging, as she had all evening though never showing concern when Zoe didn't. "She eats like the proverbial bird," her mother told Lucas. And then Lucas had said, "Do you know how much a bird eats? One of those starlings, for example? They eat something like four times their body weight in one day."

Ah Lucas, the way he looked at Zoe then, as if he knew, that sometimes she forgot she must be thinner. She forgot the terrible burden of stomach and hateful thighs, which kept you from ever being wonderful, and she ate, and having forgotten, she ate more, to forget she forgot. One hand around the damp, softening box of ice cream, in the other the spoon, hands like bird claws, eating like a bird. Her stomach danced madly as if filled with birds. Her whole body felt in motion. She strutted across her own mind, plump-chested, preening; she opened her wings and took off, soared and swooped above the balcony where Lucas, the flier, watched captivated. And then the ice cream was gone, and all that motion froze, like someone caught in the act. She looked down at her denim thighs spreading against the bed; she could barely get both hands around one. Her stomach was monstrous, almost pregnant. She was losing her shape. She would turn into one of those gross female blobs of her mother's. The thought alone was all it took to convulse her, as eyes closed above the toilet, she imagined all the birds escaping from the cage of her ribs.

Afterward she would not allow herself to sleep. Awake burned more calories, burned flesh from bones. She held one hand to the hollow of her throat and felt her heart beating fast and hot as a bird's.

THIS afternoon Zoe found her mother nestled in the wine velvet cushions of the sofa, her legs drawn up under a long Indian cotton skirt, smoking with one hand, sipping green tea with the other. From the dull puffiness of her mother's eyes, Zoe could tell she had been crying. *It is all right to cry,* Phyllis has always said. *It is a natural response of the body. Holding it back is harmful.* Zoe hates it when her mother cries, hates to see the pain, the rivulets of mascara, the surrender.

"The bus was a little late today," Zoe said, hitching the knees of her linen pants and perching on the chair opposite.

Her mother pulled herself upright, bare soles on the floor, began carefully to shift the position of everything around her—the huge pillows, ashtray, teapot, the extra cup, which she filled and handed to Zoe. "You're not happy," she told her daughter.

"I'm not?" Zoe asked, with careful laugh.

"Oh Zoe, you don't have to pretend. But why, when two people love each other, can't at least one of them be happy? You'd think they could pool their resources and work on one of them. Tell me something you want, Zoe, OK?"

"Kids my age just aren't very happy." Her mother was in one of her moods. "We grow out of it. It's no big deal."

"But what would make you happy? We could manage it."

"You must have had a bad day," Zoe said.

Phyllis took a long pull on her cigarette. "For six hours I have tried to work." She didn't exhale but let the smoke seep out as she talked. "I felt like any minute my hands were going to do something no one has ever done before, but they never did. Nothing.

I might as well have been kneading bread. At least I'd have something to show for my time."

"Let's go to the mall," Zoe suggested. She and her mother have always had a good time shopping for Zoe's clothes. When Zoe was small, her mother said, it was like having a doll. Now Zoe has her own ideas, and Phyllis, rather than objecting, seems able to guess almost infallibly what they are—sophisticated angular lines, in pastels or white and black, plenty of defining black—Phyllis combs the racks, and brings a steady supply of possibilities into the fitting room for Zoe to try. Phyllis has always shopped for herself alone and piecemeal, at craft fairs, antique markets, Episcopal church rummage sales in Leesburg, Fairfax. She's owned her favorite jacket for over twenty years—brown leather with a sunrise appliqued in faded patches and strips on the back.

"I'm going back to pots," Phyllis said dramatically. "Tomorrow I'm hooking up the wheel."

"Let's go to the mall." Zoe bounced twice in the chair to demonstrate eagerness. "I need summer things. That would make me happy."

Her mother paused, searched Zoe's face. "Lucas gets in at five," she said finally. "I think he'll be coming right over."

"Lucas?" Why the flare of panic? Zoe had not seen him since the afternoon of the roaches, assumed that like one of her mother's moods, he had passed.

"That's what he said last week before he left. He had back-to-back European runs. He said he'd be carrying his tools in the trunk of his car." Her mother's voice quavered, as if she were afraid of something too.

"What did *you* say?"

Her mother went into a prolonged shrug. "I said all right."

"Well, you must like him then," Zoe said dismissively, deciding it was all right with her, at least one of them would be happy.

"I don't know. I don't understand him. I don't know what he's after." She laughed nervously.

"Mother," Zoe said, stressing each syllable. This was no time for either one of them to act innocent.

"Do you know what he said to me? He said, Why do you

women assume that's all you've got to offer?" Phyllis shook her hair violently. "We shouldn't be talking like this."

"We always talk like this."

"I know, but."

"Don't be weird, OK? You've got to tell me what's going on." That has been, after all, Zoe's main fare—knowing. "I can handle things."

"I was asking him to spend the night."

"So?" Zoe had handled that countless times. Then all at once question and answer came together in her mind. "He didn't spend the night?" A rush of feeling, worse than any amount of fear, washed away her strength. She fell back into the chair, crushing her linen blazer.

"He said number one, it wasn't safe anymore and I should know better, and number two, that didn't matter because he'd promised himself the next time he met a woman he liked he would wait to sleep with her for six months." Her mother spoke haltingly, as though his reasoning mortified her.

"He said he liked you, anyway."

"He said he'd been through enough relationships that began with great sex. He can't afford another."

Zoe pulled herself up straight again. "Did you tell him what you think, about tapping into the flow of nature, and creating the sensuous present?"

"I can't remember," her mother said faintly, then all at once roared angrily through her teeth. "Forget him," she said, bounding up, jabbing each foot into a thong. "Let's go. He's too damned controlled. Forget him."

"I don't mind staying here and waiting to see if he shows up." Zoe's voice was playing tricks on her, first whispering and then suddenly wanting to shout. "It would be nice to have the plumbing work."

LUCAS arrived around seven, looking as if he'd never thought for a moment that he wouldn't. He was wearing fresh khakis and a white knit shirt, with the last of four neck buttons open. He had stopped somewhere to rent a giant ladder, which he had tied onto the ski-rack of his semi-restored Karmann Ghia. If there was awk-wardness in the rather formal greetings he received from mother and daughter in the front hall, he didn't seem to notice; he was more interested in introducing the two of them to his plumber's pliers, assorted wrenches, a drain snake, a staple gun, and a roll of six-inch-wide screening. He was ready to work.

"You must be hungry," Phyllis said. "I've got pastrami, Swiss cheese. A wonderful melon. Aren't you too tired for this? I mean, what time is it for you? It must be after midnight. You ought to sleep. I can make up the couch," she added quickly.

He wasn't ready to sleep. He'd spent all that time in the air dreaming of feet-on-the-ground work, making mental lists of things to do. He had promised to return the ladder the next morn-ing, and the sun was already dropping into the trees in back. "First things first," he said, unlashing the ladder from his car. He took one end, Phyllis and Zoe the other, and he led them back into the house, down the front hall, miraculously through the living room, without bumping a life-size bronze of staunchly planted legs and hips—the Arch of Triumph, he had dubbed it last week. Out on the balcony, he passed his end over the rail and took over theirs.

He dug the ladder firmly into the grass below, then produced a shoelace from his pocket and tied one end around the staple gun, the other around a belt loop. He slipped the roll of screen up his arm, swung a leg onto the ladder, and descended. When he reached the ground, he stamped his feet a few times as if to get used to it. "Come on down," he called back to them.

Zoe had never been on a ladder before, the whole thing made her think of burning buildings, great escapes. She scrambled over the edge, linen pants, Capezios and all, and breathing deep against the slight sway, carefully eased herself from rung to rung. She was afraid of losing it if she looked down, so turned her eyes on her mother's face, where she found the blank, patient expression of someone lying low.

"I think I'll use the stairs," her mother said, and disappeared. When Zoe alighted on firm ground, Lucas yanked the ladder over against the siding and extended it—halfway up the third story, barely within reach of the roof. "It's simple physics," he told Zoe, waving away her offer to steady the bottom. "It can't go anywhere." He had one foot on the first rung.

"Wait a minute, wait a minute." It was Phyllis, arms akimbo, at the open glass door.

Lucas froze, eyes front, hands in midair.

"What are you going to do?"

"I am going to staple this stuff over the vents in the soffit, to keep the birds from getting up under your eaves and building nests and shitting on your siding." It took great control for him to speak that slowly, clearly.

"And you have to do it right now? I mean, it must be two in the morning, your time."

Lucas looked at his watch and then back at Phyllis, stared at her as if he were having trouble translating her language. He didn't want to sleep, he didn't want to stop and wait for sleep to overtake him, he wanted to push himself until he dropped—at least that was what Zoe recognized.

Phyllis clenched her jaw, swallowed visibly. "I don't know whether I'm being bullied or cared for."

"Give it a while," Lucas said, "and you ought to be able to tell the difference." Unblinking, he watched her, as she appeared to consider this. Then her shoulders fell forward.

"I'll be inside," she said.

Lucas was on the ladder, his feet over Zoe's head, when she realized that she must love him. She wasn't sure why—maybe because he didn't belong to Phyllis, maybe because there was something so definite about him, but it wasn't a boyfriend sort of love. He didn't have to return it; in fact she would rather he didn't. He just had to stay there, in her life, and let her watch him while he fixed things, and she would privately love him. The ladder flexed in toward the house.

"You sure this will hold you?" she called up to him. "What if the two pieces came apart?"

"I checked everything out," he called from the higher rungs. "But thanks for your concern."

She pursed her mouth. His head and shoulders had run out of

ladder, he was stretching up, pressing the strip of screen against the eaves with the fingertips of one hand. With the other he tried to bring the staple gun into range, but he couldn't get it there: the shoelace was too short. He cursed and then tugged again, but only managed to hike his pants up on the right side where he'd tied it. The ladder shuddered, and Zoe clutched it for all she was worth.

Then Lucas climbed up one more rung. He wrapped his legs around the top rungs, twisted his right hip toward the house, and blindly felt the screen into place, firing the staple gun along its edges, clunk, clunk. He wavered precariously at each recoil. She gaped up at him in wonder, and not just his body at that odd fore-shortening angle, but his whole heroic being seemed clear to her, shining. She was still afraid he would fall, but just as sure that there was a way to fall, a way to land so you didn't get hurt, and Lucas would know what it was.

In a few minutes he was down, and without pausing to comment or change the arrangement with the inadequate shoelace, had repositioned the ladder and mounted it again. He did this three times, four. And Zoe remained dutifully at its foot, face upturned, holding him in place with her eyes.

At first she thought her ears had begun to ring from craning her neck so long. She covered and uncovered them—the noise was outside, she had never heard it start, and now it had grown in volume to something shrill and unpleasant. Beyond the cluster of town-houses to the south, a long cloud of black birds hung in the pale violet sky. They were their own fixed path, funneling in from the invisible distance, spreading to rest in the saved trees at the base of the back slope. The shrieking came from the trees: when you looked closely among the leaves, it was as if each branch was thick with black fruit. Zoe had never seen anything like it.

When Lucas came down to move the ladder for the last time, she said, "They don't like what we're doing." It did seem their shrieking was directed at the two of them. "Maybe they think you've caught one of their friends up there behind the screen," Zoe said, to be amusing, but Lucas said it was just what starlings did, gather for the night in communal roosts. They had probably been there every night since early spring, carrying on, making a mess. She had just never noticed it.

"I guess I'd rather sleep up there under our roof where I could get comfortable than have to balance all night on a tree branch," said Zoe.

"Starlings are the roaches of the bird world," Lucas called down meaningfully as he climbed one last time. A few minutes later he was finished, sliding the ladder back to carrying size with loud clanks.

"Could you see whether they'd built a nest or something?" Zoe asked.

"Didn't look," Lucas said.

"Probably they hadn't yet." She gazed skeptically at the streaks and blotches on the siding.

"Hard to say. It is that time of year. You know," Lucas went on, "being a pilot, there's no love lost between myself and birds. I could tell you a story or two about the accidents they've caused, hitting propellers, getting sucked into jet engines, gumming up the works. A couple years ago out of JFK a bunch of gulls sailed right up into one of my engines two minutes after takeoff."

"That's so sad."

"I don't know about sad. The way a jet turbine works, it's got these finely balanced blades. A bird carcass gets in there and the engine chokes up." Zoe made a little gagging sound. "Look," Lucas said, "that engine was ruined. I had to fly out over the Atlantic and dump 100,000 pounds of fuel before that jumbo was light enough to land minus an engine. That's megabucks down the drain, not to mention the danger. When you look at it that way, it's them or us."

Zoe could tell that she was being tested. She wasn't supposed to waste sympathy on the gulls, act squeamish at their fate. That was all right. She could see that a jumbo jet was more important than a handful of birds. Lucas was realistic. How much he knew about certain things! Clear, definite knowledge. She searched her mind for something comparably definite to say, something to suggest she was in agreement with him on the issue of birds. But all that came to mind in that driving clamor of bird screams was a jumble of her mother's pronouncements, bitter and nebulous as a mouthful of smoke.

LUCAS has showered in Zoe's tub and crashed on the sofa, which Phyllis fixed up for him. There was nothing for mother and daughter to do then but retire early to their own rooms upstairs and downstairs, leaving him the middle. Was it because Lucas was watching that Zoe hugged her mother before they parted, something she never does willingly, unless for a camera? And why her mother's body seemed so sadly appealing to her arms, her mother's odd scorched smell, so suddenly sweet, Zoe doesn't know.

Zoe won't be able to eat tonight because she doesn't dare try to sneak by Lucas. That is all right. She would much rather know he is stationed there at the center of the house, a guardian of order. Stomach clenched around its treasured pain, she lies awake thinking about this man—his determination on the ladder, the way he thanked her for her concern. She goes over and over these moments in her mind, savoring them. She imagines that she has emptied herself in order to be filled more purely and perfectly by his image. When she closes her eyes, he is all she sees, poised at the foot of the ladder, then at different stages of his ascent. *Give it a while,* he keeps telling her, and she knows that he does what he does because he cares.

He has climbed far above her now, and the ladder keeps lengthening. He is climbing far beyond the roof of the house, so far she can hardly see him. Her stomach begins to ache with worry. Then the dreadful noise begins—she knows even while it is dim and distant, it is dreadful. She tries to call a warning to Lucas, but he is too high to hear, and soon the noise is deafening, and the sky darkens with enemy starlings. Lucas is engulfed by a black cloud of them; Zoe screams as loud as she can, but nothing can be heard over that noise. Then as she looks up, something comes sliding down the ladder, something shapeless, shrunken lands at her feet. She wakes up in terror, the noise still in her ears.

She must calm herself. She is awake now. She is safe inside.

There are no birds, they are are all asleep in the trees, balancing somehow on their branches without falling.

But that noise still shrieks in her ears, and she must make sure. She turns on the light and stumbles to the window, pulls the drape aside, tries to peer beyond the glass, through the reflection of her own room, her own body, all arms and legs, wrapped in a large men's T-shirt.

She is awake now, yet it seems the noise has filled her room, and she drags open the glass door to let it out. The night air flows in, chills her into alertness. The noise inside dissipates, met as it is by another sound from above, beyond the screen, softer, but as shrill and relentless, the sort of sound, like crickets, or running water, you could confuse with silence unless you'd been warned it was there.

Square Zero

RAFE wouldn't let it alone. Their dogs, a pair of chocolate labs, were like *family,* he said, giving me that suppliant public defender look of his. Where was my Christmas *spirit?* Old Moose might not have another year left in him, and Godiva adored festive gatherings. Didn't I see? They were the children he and Noah would never have. I'd never dream of excluding Betsy, would I?

"Betsy has never run around the house out of control," I said. "Not even as a child."

But argue with Rafe long enough and you begin to feel selfish, sleazy, right wing. Finally I said, *For heaven's sake, bring them along, there's always room at the inn*—a generous sentiment that comes back to haunt me now, as two large spoiled canines burst into my tiny front hall, Rafe and Noah squeezing after them. Rafe's eyes tear with pride as Godiva rises onto her hind legs and backs me into an abrupt seat on the stairs. "She's so happy. She wants to thank you," Rafe says, his hands clasped under his chin.

19

"Grab her, for godsake," says Noah. He's got his arms around a huge pot of the leek soup he promised and a bottle of wine in one fist. Godiva gallops into the living room, her nails clicking and scratching on the bare floor.

Noah jerks his foot so Old Moose will get off it, then we all make our way out to the kitchen, where Betsy looks up from yesterday's crossword. "Oh hi," she says, flipping aside her long pale waves, Alice-in-Wonderland hair she should probably cut now that she's graduated. She grabs it almost cruelly in one fist, thrusts it behind her, but as she bends again over the puzzle, it slides forward to curtain her face. The back of her rumpled Bryn Mawr sweatshirt celebrates 100 YEARS OF CASTRATING BITCHES.

"Oh hi," Noah says reproducing her tone. "I'm just the guy with the soup."

"I basted the turkey," Betsy says. It sits now on the counter while its juices settle, a mountain of foil, the only absolute in this revision of Christmas past. I was adamant with Noah when I went next door to invite them: we were keeping the food light this year, simple, digestible, low-profile—a variety of salads, steamed vegetables. Fruit for after.

"Where is your Christmas spirit?" he protested in turn. He is Jewish and doesn't like to see the opposing traditions tampered with. "We want eggnog, we want candied sweet potatoes and gravy and figgy pudding, we want—"

I made as if to block his mouth with my hand. He is not the most sensitive of men, but how could he be? An immunologist at NIH, he describes his research in military metaphors—offensives, body counts—and on bad days his sense of humor runs like an open wound. Like last week he told Rafe and me it was time he cut some sort of deal with the Powers That Be—his life in exchange for one clear piece of the HIV puzzle, preferably a piece with Nobel potential. It was after work and we were out in our adjoining backyards. Noah stooped for the Frisbee Godiva had dropped at his feet, then flung it into the dark. Rafe, who's never sure Noah isn't serious, pleaded with him not to tempt fate; Noah accused Rafe of blindness—worse, indifference—to the big picture. "All he's worried about," Noah told me, stooping again, flinging, "is saving his own personal ass."

I have no big picture, just discrete shots. Noah's elfin smile once he gets to Rafe. Rafe's milky blue eyes when they glimpse the danger in loving too much. Frisbees flying away; Frisbees returning between the jaws of sacred dogs. And popping up through them all, the one of Betsy, after spending Thanksgiving with her father, calling to me from the bathroom floor around midnight—drenched with sweat, still heaving emptily. Food totally stressed her out, she said between sobs, she couldn't deal with food.

Home the next morning from the emergency room, her fluids replenished, she slept angelically for most of the day. I stumbled over to Rafe and Noah's back porch, I was in their kitchen raving: *I have no idea what I'm supposed to do. Follow her around every time she eats? Food is food. Who's ever heard of not being able to deal with it—you* have *to let it stay in your stomach, become part of you. It's absurd to think you have any choice.* I couldn't keep myself from crying in front of them. *What have I done wrong?*

Rafe fussed at the stove with a mug of tea for me, plunked in two spoonfuls of sugar before I could stop him. "She did reach out to you," he said, bowing more than he had to to wrap my fingers around the mug handle. "She could have kept you in the dark."

Perched on a chrome stool, Noah's response was to tell us about his mother's thing with butter-almond ice cream, how she would go through a whole half gallon in one episode of *My Little Margie* right from the carton. He mimed the hypnotic dipping of the demurely held spoon, the wide stare. "Afterward she burped into her napkin, called it a touch of indigestion and disappeared into the john. Look," he promised, "it's not going to kill her." Where there are no enemy germs, there is nothing to culture, nothing to cure.

Tonight I help Noah peel off each sleeve of his down parka while he stirs the warming soup. He is wearing charcoal pleated pants and a crisp mint green button-down.

"Fancy, shmancy," Betsy says with a twitch of a smile, an unexpected gift that lifts my spirits. I've wished she'd relax with Rafe and Noah, treat them as family, but she doesn't really know them, having already gone off to college when they moved out of the city to Takoma Park. It was just when I'd given up on meeting new men—I was tired of forcing such alertness after a day of work, tired of dreaming clichés, the prospect of growing old alone had begun to glimmer like an exotic holiday—when they appeared, the two of them, staggering back and forth from U-Haul to house, tripping over dogs. Their neighbor on Capitol Hill had been robbed of the trash he was taking out, robbed and then shot, right beside his own back gate. Noah could think of better ways to die.

Now he gives Betsy a little nod, his eyes crinkling to slits behind his wire-rims, and pats his ribs affectionately. "There's a stick of butter in the soup," he whispers to me. "And heavy cream."

I won't rise to the bait. I am too pleased at this moment with the way his hair folds thick as thatch over his ears.

"You didn't say we couldn't wear jeans." There is Rafe, taking up the kitchen doorway, painting that pout of his with Chapstick. Eight years younger than Noah and me and so unreasonably tall, he needs constant reassurance. He has round cheeks and dark blond unruly hair, and when he skips a shave, looks like a giant child with smudges on his face.

"As long as they're clean," I say, knowing he is obsessed with laundry, does a small load every evening, wastes water, drives Noah crazy.

"As if clean were an option," says Noah. "Talk about denial."

"Shut up," Rafe says.

Betsy sets down her pencil. "You guys better be nice."

"Of course we'll be nice," I say.

"We're always nice," says Rafe, turning one shoulder forward.

Noah pauses in his stirring to take a noisy sip from the spoon, plunks it back into the pot, and dares us to object. He is always ready to deliver his losing-battle speech on microbes—their power and numbers versus the frail and futile dream of antisepsis ("picture the Kennedy Center packed with cockroaches, and you've got one can of Raid").

"Actually why should I care *how* you guys act? It's not like you're my children or anything." Betsy draws herself up out of the chair to her full height—such a glorious spectacle I can't not believe—the way she tucks the pencil into that cloud of hair, stretches an arm toward the ceiling and yawns to the jingle of earrings, bracelets. Why dwell on a gray, turned-away face, limp hands, an IV dripping into one wrist?

Betsy is doing fine these days, I tell her father, when he calls to imply that any problems she might have are my fault. I could have devoted more time to Betsy, he says, could have helped her identify practical career goals, prevented the burn-out she has come home to recover from, if I hadn't been so busy crusading for all womankind. He has been a partner in a Richmond law firm for years now and likes to make fun of affirmative action, my specialty; he knows and I know it's just another way to push paper.

Betsy is doing fine, we have decided, Noah, Rafe, and I. Vaguely embarrassed, I went to her bedside, took her hand; she offered vague promises to take better care of herself. My mind a turmoil of questions, I grasped at one. "Does it have something to do with Philip?" If anyone merited suspicion, it was this person Philip, whom she'd started seeing the month before.

"Does what?" she asked.

"The business with food," I said.

Her face softened into a look of supreme pity. "Poor Mom," she said. "It's not something I can just explain. I'm *really* sorry though for adding to your worries."

"What worries?" She flinched at my rising voice. "I don't have any worries," I said more calmly.

"I think Philip is probably good for me," she said after a moment. "It's almost more than I can stand."

"I hope this Philip dude understands one thing," chef Noah tells us now. "No honorable intentions, no soup."

Betsy gazes at him with her special combination of polite respect and disapproval; he becomes involved with the contents of his pot.

"What is it with these cookbooks?" he says. "I mean, you follow the recipe, trust it implicitly, and you get to the end and it says

Correct the seasoning. So what do they think you've put in all that time and energy for? To wind up with the wrong seasoning? And then they leave you to fix it by yourself."

Philip must have let himself in, because all at once Rafe has stepped into the kitchen: he is looking down his shoulder at the stranger who has come from behind and replaced him in the door frame, who seems particularly small compared to gigantic Rafe, much smaller than I have been picturing him. *Men,* Betsy calls her contemporaries. But this is a boy.

His deep-set eyes, light gray, move from one of us to another, brimming with anxious appeal. He is wearing a white shirt, newly unfolded, and a red tie flecked with something green. Betsy has gone flushed and clumsy, stumbles in her long skirt and open black hightops. We wait for her to reach him and plant a formal kiss on the mouth he manages to hold still though he is batting Godiva away from his crotch with one hand and trying not to drop the pot of white chrysanthemums he proffers with the other.

FOR the two days before he gave Betsy a call, Philip was a heartless and thus desirable man. He had turned up at a Halloween party she almost stayed home from, feeling herself to be what he obliviously was—alien, unconnected, the one who just didn't belong in that web of college friends and their housemates. The weekend before, at the Takoma Park Third World Jamboree, a woman had plaited Betsy's hair into a mop of beaded cornrows as a public demonstration, which inspired the costume I helped her assemble that night—an old pair of organdy curtains, a wide silver belt, and assorted jewelry—"Fertility goddess or vestal virgin," I said, "take your pick."

"This whole thing is so absurd," she kept saying, trying not to pay attention to the image taking shape in the full-length mirror.

"It will probably be good for you to see some people your own age," I said. "Just relax and enjoy yourself."

"You'd like that, wouldn't you?" she said smoothly.

"Of course, I would. I want you to be happy."

She jerked herself out of the mirror, away from where I knelt with my needle and thread. "So you can be rid of me," she said.

"Betsy, for heaven's sake, no," I said, flushing the way I do when I lie. "That's not how I feel. I'm concerned about your future, certainly, but—"

"That's OK, Mom," she interrupted, putting herself back in my hands. "It was a joke."

I resumed my stitching. "Please don't joke about things like that."

She patted my head. "I'm sorry," she said. She began poking through the collection of little boxes on her bureau. "Look," she said, producing an old silver turquoise ring of her father's and slipping it on her big toe. "The finishing touch." A snort of rare laughter escaped her, then she drew in her smile, and went off to cross paths with Philip, who claimed to have gotten lost on his way to some other gathering. He had been drawn to the lights, the strains of Talking Heads and laughter spilling out into the street. When Betsy discovered him, he was in the kitchen eating one of the apples someone had thought they might bob for, chewing and talking real estate with several of the young men: the money to be made if you had the guts to move into the city's marginal neighborhoods— Logan Circle, Meridian Hill.

Did I know how guys could be when they got together like that, Betsy wanted to know? "It's like they've all agreed to play grown up and pretend they've got interesting jobs, and light each other's cigarettes."

I could get the picture, I told her, wondering was there really a difference between playing grown up and being grown up? The possibility was a luxury I'd never been able to afford.

Apparently Philip was not like the others. That night there were three of them—a Count Dracula, a Diogenes, and a pepper mill— and they drank their Michelobs and computed appreciation percentages while Philip chomped away on his apple, core and all, and changed the subject whenever he got a chance to things like knocking down extraneous walls, exposing brick, replacing pipes. The discussion went on this way in parallel tracks until Betsy gathered the nerve to break in. "What about the displaced families?" she blurted, and of course all the other guys stared at her, questioning her right to speak.

But Philip told her not to worry about displaced families; he was thinking of *condemned* houses, *abandoned* property, the families long gone. "I'm talking about starting from square zero," he said. Then he said a friend of his had had her hair done like Betsy's and when she finally unbraided it, it all fell out.

NOAH is at the head of the table now by virtue of his soup, which he ladles into our bowls. I am at the other end nearest the kitchen, dissecting the turkey and trying to avoid staring at Betsy and Philip to my right—the way he keeps checking her prim profile. He rests his hand on the back of her chair, and every time he lets it touch her hair, thick and golden as ever, I wince—I don't know why. Is she tilting her head very slightly into his hand, or politely shrugging it off?

Lately she has been rude to him on the phone—I have held my breath, straining to catch her side of the conversation. I want to know what's going on. Yesterday she told me the four-room cracker box Philip rents beyond the Beltway is falling apart, one maintenance emergency after another, and all he can think about is digging a basement. He is working out a deal with his landlord, has a book on the subject with diagrams, and wonders if she, Betsy, will help him. Is that so unforgivable? Is it so terrible to go out in the morning to pick up bagels for breakfast and return two and a half hours later with a sack of dented and day-old groceries plus a story about giving a guy who was wandering around stoned and freezing a ride to the Salvation Army? Meanwhile she was starving, she said. The word hung in the air between us like an awkward question.

I must remind myself of certainties—this is my house, my turkey, both bought with my well-earned paychecks, these are my dear friends, this is today. My life, if not complete, has at least achieved a sort of poise, an adjustment of expectations. Now and then there comes a thud on the door to the basement, where Godiva has been stashed; on my left, Rafe, her overruled advocate, is coating his mouth with Chapstick and sulking. Stretched out under the table, usurping foot room, Old Moose farts mercilessly.

In his Julia Child voice, Noah is recounting the saga of his Christmas Eve, a story that permits him finally to point out that he had to hit four different stores before he could take enough leeks for the soup. After that he doesn't dare raise his eyes from his bowl, concentrates on strident sips from his spoon.

"There weren't more than half a dozen cars on the roads," Philip says. "And nobody just out walking along the sidewalks. It was weird. Like a nuclear attack or something."

"Most people are already where they want to be by Christmas." I am sure that sounded like an accusation, not the harmless filler I intended. I regret the look that crosses Philip's face, so pink and raw from its recent shave, doubt mixed with a willingness to endure whatever barbs I may aim at him.

"Good soup," he says graciously. There is a white film along his upper lip that needs wiping. Betsy has done nothing but drag a spoon through hers.

"One of these years, I'm going to grow leeks in the backyard," I say, groping for a fresh start. He may be good for Betsy, he may not, but I have nothing against him personally. "I know it's supposed to be tricky but what's there to lose?"

"It *is* tricky," Philip says. "I never had any luck with leeks. Couldn't get them to come up ever, leeks."

"*You* couldn't?" I ask. He is looking through me with that forced blankness of someone who has just lied. "I mean, you *couldn't?*" The last thing I want is the complication of catching him.

"In 4-H. When I was a kid." He is worrying the chunk of dark bread on his side plate into crumbs.

Noah stares at him over his wire rims. "There's really such a thing as 4-H?" Noah grew up in Brooklyn Heights. Went to N.Y.U.

"It's not just a bunch of Republican propaganda?" says Rafe.

"Don't leeks have a long growing season?" I ask, seriously.

"Very long," admits Philip.

"And don't they need special soil?"

"Mother," Betsy says. "You don't have to try so hard."

But I do. Philip must believe that I believe that as a child he tried to grow leeks.

"Well, yes. It's basically sand," Philip says, conquering a stammer, his eyes darting from Betsy to my shirt buttons. "Basically you plant in sand in the fall and harvest the following summer. That is, if anything comes up."

"Remember Zucchiniland?" Rafe asks dreamily.

"Lahnd," Noah corrects, "Zucchinilahnd."

Betsy does not remember, though she isn't going to give anyone an opening by saying so. She spent most of last summer at her father's place in Nags Head, and I never happened to tell her about the two zucchini seeds I planted out by the back fence.

But Philip dutifully asks and Noah explains how the two vines produced squash so prolifically that we three neighbors began to fall prey to delusions of grandeur. As they piled up in our refrigerators and on our kitchen window sills, we imagined erecting a six-foot stockade around our properties and seceding from the United States—the Democrats were getting to be as bad as the Republicans, after all. Noah was to be in charge of Health and Welfare; Rafe would say good-bye to his thankless job of keeping all the schizoid vagrants in D.C. out of jail and dictate Justice. And by virtue of my amazing gift for agriculture, I would be in charge of exports—basically zucchini, though Rafe thought he might do some research on creating compost from dog shit. We had just made a final decision on our flag—two green squash in a circular design reminiscent of yin and yang—when both plants began to shrivel from the center out. We watered them twice a day, and applied Miracle Gro, but by the end of the week they and the ideal state of Zucchinilahnd had withered away.

Philip gives out a hearty laugh that ends as abruptly as it began. Betsy's lip line softens slightly, almost a smile. We are coming through something, I think. We are all trying—you have to try a little in situations like this, even when it doesn't feel right, there is nothing wrong with having to try. Maybe Betsy is realizing that. As a child, she used to cover the bottom of her face with her hands and ask me, "Guess if I'm smiling or angry," holding her eyes neutral, deceptive. She is still a mystery to me; she is taking great care with the arrangement of different foods on her plate, little bits of this and that which she prods tentatively, curiously with her fork.

These last weeks, she has asked me for history—the apartments we lived in before this house (she remembers haunted laundry rooms, threatening trashmen, a colony of roaches invading her candy collection); the injuries she suffered, a broken finger (she remembers how it smelled when the cast came off, odor of rot no soap could wash away), twelve stitches in her chin (at the sight of the needle, she wet her pants). We have reviewed the times I left her with my parents to go off with a *new friend* to the Eastern Shore, the Virgin Islands, Greece, and she has asked me why. "I was searching for something," I've told her, "something that didn't exist," and she gave me the oddest look, sorrowful and bored, as if to say, *I could have told you that. Why didn't you ask?*

When I wondered what she was thinking, she's said, "I'm thinking that I'd do anything not to make your mistakes."

"It hasn't all been mistakes," I said. "I have no desire to go back and undo anything." Looking bored again, she said she knew that—but I *had* lied to her.

"You *promised* me you weren't going to get a divorce."

"I'm sure I didn't think we would when I promised that. We were working on the marriage, Betsy. I thought we were making progress."

"And you just thought wrong," she said.

"Not wrong," I said, keeping my voice calm. "But it got harder and harder. And then one day we couldn't work anymore." I could never tell her that it was practically an accident, a tip of the scales. One day, his urge to leave was stronger than my urge to stop him.

But here, now, there is earnest Philip, a good sign. I watch Betsy watch him scoop large servings of green salad and apple-yogurt salad onto the base of turkey slabs on his plate, add struts of broccoli, a layer of beans. Does she remember her outrage as a child when there were "things touching things" on her plate?

Philip is about to fork a large combination bite into his mouth, when Rafe says, "I'm assuming you're a liberal. I can usually tell when someone isn't—it's like the lack of compassion causes a certain smell." Philip puts down his fork, sits back in his chair, smiles and nods unconvincingly. "You haven't told us what you do. Noah's a doctor, I'm a lawyer."

Philip musters his forces. "Would you believe Indian chief?" He produces another loud laugh, which I try to pick up. Then he adds, tentatively, "My father says I'm a businessman." He isn't sure we will see that that is much the better joke.

"Fathers are all the same," Rafe says. "They want capitalists. They want quarterbacks. They want you dead with a Silver Star."

"So are you or are you not in business?" asks Noah. Why does he always have to be as harsh as Rafe is sympathetic?

Philip steals a look at Betsy and all at once I am longing for her to return it, to smile at him, for the two of them to promise something silly—to cling to each other in the face of hardship and danger. In the face of us, who are so worn out and shrewd. Maybe he detects some shift in her mood in his favor, for he looks directly at Noah and says, "I'm a telemarketer. I sell accounting systems to small businesses on commission. I sit for eight but really ten hours a day in an office but really a cell with a phone and a computer terminal." His voice has become more assured, forceful. "I'm good at it. They're always naming me Marketer of the Month, and giving me bonuses and stuff. And I hate every fucking minute."

Betsy's gaze swings around to me—this is what she has been trying to tell me, the way jobs are; did I want to condemn her to such torture? Noah shrugs. Rafe, bless him, has gone wide-eyed with compassion. Slumping back into a boyish blur, Philip sets about consuming the food on his plate in large bites.

Betsy picks up hers, half-empty, and takes it into the kitchen. I feel compelled to follow, to clear something up, though I don't know what it can be. I watch her scrape the food she needs into the trash. "You know," I find myself whispering, "he reminds me of someone."

Betsy raises her brow noncommittally.

"Something around the eyes," I say, thinking, *the muddle of hunger and fear;* thinking, *it is written all over each of us, like different maps to the same place.*

"Could you maybe chill a little?" Betsy says.

"I am chilled," I tell her, reminding myself, *Philip looks like Philip. Betsy and Philip will cling to each other. Betsy is going to be fine.* "But I think he's nice." I lower my voice. "I wasn't at all sure I'd like him, but I *do*. I just wanted to tell you that."

To my surprise, her face opens, expectant.

"He certainly isn't pretentious." What does it say about someone that he has tried more than once to grow leeks? "He cares about you, Betsy." I am embarrassed that my voice is hoarse.

Her blue eyes go dull, unreadable. She says, "What difference does that make?"

I want to tell her that Philip needs her now, that she needs him, that I see it so clearly I could cry. "Maybe I'm just trying to say that you shouldn't worry so much about making mistakes."

She straightens her posture and raises her chin so that she can look down on me more. "You're trying to pawn me off on him." I start to protest but she puts her hand on my mouth. "It's OK, you can't help it. You had to get married. It makes you anxious that I'm not weighed down at this age the way I weighed you down."

"Betsy," I say, half-shocked, half-chiding, loud enough to cause a lull in the murmuring in the other room. I put my mouth to her ear. "I wanted to have you. You know that."

"I'm sorry," she says, shaking her head, tucking up one side of her mouth—she is not so foolish as to believe me. "You must have just wanted to die."

"I give up!" I don't care who hears me. "I'm tired of your putting words in my mouth. I mention that I think Philip is nice, and the next thing I know, you're telling me—"

"If you think he's so wonderful, why don't *you* marry him?" she says as she disappears into the dining room.

I return to my seat and for a long moment there is only the sound of Godiva's claws on the basement door.

"Welcome back," Noah says finally, blandly. "We've been torturing Philip here to confess what he got for Christmas."

Betsy is at the window, staring out; offshoots of the hanging spider plant dangle about her shoulders. Philip looks terribly embarrassed and sad above his jaunty tie.

"Betsy gave me these," I say, fingering the hoops of bone in my ears. "And I gave her those." She is wearing the identical pair, souvenirs of that easy afternoon at the Third World Jamboree. "Amazing, isn't it? Neither of us knew the other had picked them out."

Philip nods too hard, finally stops and blurts, "Well, I guess my folks sent me a muffler, basically, and a monogrammed box to hold floppy disks."

The dullness of it depresses us further. "You guess," says Noah after a heavy pause.

"We're not that close," Philip says.

Noah drains his wineglass. "That isn't even funny, floppy disks."

"Since when does everything have to be funny?" Betsy asks, turning into the room abruptly.

The grin freezes on Noah's face. Rafe hangs his head like Godiva after you scold her. "Not everything," Noah says. "But a *soupçon* of funny now and then, to correct the seasoning."

"So you can forget what a bitch life is?" The blood rises into Betsy's cheeks. "So you guys can pretend you've found happiness with each other, and your politically correct jobs, and she can forget everything she did and say it was all for the best and act like the perfect mother now? Well, I'm not going to forget. I think it's *immoral*." Philip puts one arm out to catch her waist and draw her to him, and for a moment's innocence, she lets him hold her, rest his head against her flank. Then she twists away.

"I happen to think it's immoral to go crazy," Noah says.

"I am not going crazy," Betsy says haughtily.

"I meant me," Noah says, "if I didn't laugh."

Betsy goes quiet. Godiva, who particularly overreacts to raised voices, is now yelping and throwing herself against the door. Then Betsy says, "I'm very sorry"—her voice trembles—"I'm really *very* sorry, but I just do hate all of you."

Philip's face collapses; I jump up from my seat.

"You may be mildly depressed," Rafe says. "It's not your fault, you realize."

"I guess I can handle that," Noah says at the same time. "The vast majority of Americans hate me. You might as well add your little dose."

Betsy opens her mouth but no words come out. As if she has

glimpsed something scary, she plunges out of the room with a throaty groan. From the hall there comes the jangling of hangers and then the front door opens and slams shut.

We are too stunned to look at each other. I feel this strange need to apologize profusely, abjectly, but Rafe and Noah would only make light of it. They will do whatever they have to do to make me feel better, instantly forgiving me everything, knowing me not at all. And I can't stand to acknowledge the hurt on Philip's face.

"She's always doing that," Philip says finally.

My brain echoes with all the answers: *Doing what? Oh, that. That's nothing. Don't pay any attention to that. Betsy's going to be fine.* "I know," I tell Philip, and the floor starts slipping out from under my feet, like sand after a broken wave. Maybe it's Betsy I owe apologies—the idea overwhelms me and I have to sit down.

"I think she's depressed," Rafe says again. "I can give you the name of my therapist." When no one responds, he shoves his balled napkin into his mouth.

"I'll go after her," Philip says. "Sometimes that works."

"Time for dessert," Noah says. "What are you hiding out there? Pumpkin pie with whipped cream? Plum pudding and hard sauce?"

"Maybe if we both," I tell Philip, who gives Rafe and Noah a nod, and sort of escapes into the front hall.

"Well, I'm going to let poor Godiva out," Rafe says huffily. "While you guys are off taking care of Betsy, she could be having herself a nice little pee."

All of us but Noah have crowded into the foyer, we are pulling parkas from the closet, struggling into them, dragging Godiva out of the way of the opening door. Then in a flash Godiva has burst outside, she goes careening around the yard, barking her defiance of us who locked her up. None of us moves to follow because at the center of the dog's circles, Betsy stands on the flagstone path to the street, hugging her man's overcoat around her. She is facing the house and crying. Godiva goes into a crouch near Betsy, paws the grass, and barks and barks.

"She wants you to play," Rafe calls, but Betsy shows no sign of hearing.

Then Philip crosses the threshold and starts down the three

front steps, cautiously, for he is injured himself and she might get frightened and run. When he reaches the path, she seems to recognize him, and then Rafe and me still on the porch. She tries to smile up at us as she cries, raises one hand in a sort of wave, calls, "I don't know where I go from here."

Figure Drawing

MARSH doesn't lift weights or diet or jog, he doesn't pay any attention to his body at all, which is maybe why Ana had to possess it, trace its contours, make them speak. It wasn't about sex, or rather sex was the least of it, the easy part. If formal portraits are her meal ticket, the body has always been her avocation, her secret stash, her wine. And his was an instant high. She wanted to draw it in every conceivable pose, never let it out of her sight. She assumed such a desire meant love.

Their courtship was packaged adventure, sea kayaking off the coast of Maine, canoeing the boundary waters, trekking horseback into the Black Hills. "Yes," said Ana cheerfully, heroically, because she sensed Marsh was testing her. "*Yes.*" She swam laps, walked miles: she was tougher than she looked. She would prove herself, follow him anywhere. She would take her sketchbook, which she would fill with gestures, action studies, which would inspire a burst of original paintings, her own show: The Mystery of the Male. But she came back with mostly blank pages. There was never time to draw. She was too busy enduring saddle sores, yeast infections, insect bites, aches in the muscles and joints that would continue for weeks afterward. She worried that she might not survive.

Right now they could have been honeymooning in the Costa Rican jungle, tagging frogs. Or dog-sledding in the Rockies—so much hardship, so little time. Except that finally she could push aside the brochures, lean her face into his, and muster her most urgent appeal: "Let's try something tranquil for once." He gave her a complicated look—*what have I gotten myself into?* But Ana was the last person he could ask. Then he squared his shoulders— he would do tranquillity with the same determination that he had done everything else.

A TAP-TAP on the door of their villa, which Marsh swears he locked, and the next minute they hear the screen slide. The woman almost catches them, she may have been expecting to, maybe all pale North Americans awaken their first morning in the mood. In one easy motion Marsh rolls off the bed, pulls on his swim trunks, and saunters out into the living room, while Ana scrambles for the bathroom, embarrassed as a teenager with a reputation at stake.

Mistress Crawford is tall and stately, with square shoulders and a handshake as firm as a man's. Her sun-streaked hair is pulled back tight from her high, round brow into a bun.

"Your first visit to the island?" she says in a deep voice. "Bet you enjoy it. You will come back again. It's very friendly place, very honest."

"Like a painting," Ana says, gazing at the sea beyond the verandah, thinking, *This is what they mean by light.* A luminous turquoise deepens in the distance to a Prussian blue banded by the rise of a neighboring landmass, the misty purple of a bruise. It cries out for watercolors at least, and she has brought only pencil and pen.

"Always a breeze." Mistress Crawford goes about opening all the sliding glass. The air swirls pleasantly. "Don't have to close nothing. Nobody going to take nothing. Island people very honest," she promises Marsh, who has got the coffee brewing and is watching it drip into the carafe. Then she turns to Ana. "I have five children, all girls. All have names with J." Her skin is a warm brown, her face kindly, though a permanent squint all but hides her eyes and she keeps her upper lip stretched over the gaps in her teeth. Ana hears Jasmine, Jamaica, Jezebel, the invitation to share; sees the impatience in Marsh's arms braced on the counter, his hunched back. Man quietly defending his privacy.

"Our children are all grown-up now," Ana says, as if the exaggeration might justify vaguely dismissing them.

"Time for grandchildren then," Mistress Crawford says.

"Maybe someday." His back flexes. Her daughter Lauren, lost to a dream of wealth, has risen from selling vitamins to teaching others to sell vitamins for her. Chris, her artistic one, keeps changing his major and puncturing his poor body with rings and garish tattoos, but he remains sober, which is all Ana dare hope, sober and alive. Marsh's son, Mike, was much decorated in Boy Scouts and is studying to be an engineer like Marsh. He directs most of what he has to say to his father, and shyly calls Ana *ma'am*.

Abruptly Marsh turns into the conversation, picks up a map on the counter. "Hey, where's the best coral around here?" he says with an aggressive smile. Mistress Crawford takes the map uncertainly, holds it sideways, then tries upside down. "Which beach?" he goes on. "If we're planning to swim out and see all the fish."

She leads him outside, waves way down the shoreline, draws specific directions in the air endlessly. He thanks her, then suggests that since they have been in the villa barely twelve hours, she can let any housekeeping go until tomorrow morning.

"My entire life I live on this island," she says as she leaves, "and never once do I swim out and see all the fish."

MARSH is down on his knees like a dog, clawing a hole in the sand for the umbrella pole, its depth based on some principle of physics. "There's no way I'm calling a woman Mistress anything," he says. "We'll get going earlier tomorrow—be gone by the time she arrives."

Ana settles back into the shade. The temperature of the air is perfect, like silk sliding over her skin. Her bones go soft. They have bumped over pocked road, through herds of goats, passed more rusted hunks of car and half-built, crumbling concrete structures than she cares to count. But now her gaze opens wide on water and sky, drinks in the lush, fertile light. An occasional pinkish body crosses in front of her, and her drawing hand twitches in response, but against that depth of background most look like boring little machines, their spirits choked by self-consciousness or layers of fat.

Marsh fidgets. He unfolds his map across his thighs, refolds it, flexes his calves. "I'm trying to figure out," he says after a while, "if the dark spot off that point is more reef or just weeds."

She leans over and rubs her cheek along the curve of his biceps. "What is it about breasts?" she asks.

"What is what?" He follows her nod in the direction of one young woman she might have sketched, evenly brown except for the wedge of cloth at her groin. Propped on an arm planted in the sand, she sits reading, her legs bent to the side, a study in subtle tensions, the body twisting to receive sun. She can feel Marsh's cells vibrate. *That.* He's an arrow, her nipples two bull's eyes.

"In class when we start on the nude and the girl disrobes, everyone freezes. How come? How come all they can do is gape?"

Marsh smiles obligingly. "I don't see any great mystery there."

"But it's different with the guy. The G-string comes off and everyone gets very busy with their pencils—all eyes studiously avoiding the key part. In a lot of their early drawings it isn't even there."

His smile gets fixed. "That's interesting," he says. "Now I say we start over here." He waves his hand in the other direction. "Swim out just beyond the reef, then let the current do most of the work."

She pulls herself up with a sigh, removes her hat, dark glasses. Whatever it is they are running from, she and her husband, they have been rescued for a time by two pairs of flippers and two masks. "I'm worried about all these nipples," she says as she trudges behind him to the point of entry he has picked. "Whether it doesn't raise the risk of cancer to expose them to such strong sun."

MOST of her students at the community college speak with accents. The families of some have emigrated from the islands; others come from El Salvador, Cambodia, Ghana, Iran. Their search for a better life has led them to choose marketing as a major. They add figure drawing as an elective, not because they have the passion to create or because they view careful, heartfelt attention to the human form as a meaningful or even sane enterprise but because the average grade in the course is B.

She shouldn't judge them. Who's to say she ever had it herself, the passion? Maybe it was just patience, the willingness to work a picture until it was right; instead of genius, simply the understanding that art takes time. And how much time can a person afford?

She doesn't remember when it stopped being enough, the deep concentration, the presence of something afterward that wasn't there before. Maybe she just wanted that presence to make a difference to someone besides herself, maybe that is why she has settled for making portraits in exchange for large, appreciative fees. Painting by numbers—it almost is, when you consider the limits of varia tions of the human skull and the fact that most subjects are paying to look the same—eyes a tad larger and wider apart, jaws firmer, noses smaller, ears more laid back, hairlines less. Plastic surgery for the mind's eye. She has made a small name.

Marsh likes to say that he is a teacher too—his students are missiles and bombs which must be trained to ferret out targets with great accuracy, to slip down smokestacks, zero in on other missiles, distinguish between a hangar full of fighter jets and a school full of kids. He is often called upon to brief official contingents from Europe. Like a pleased parent, he documents his weapons' achievements with videos and photographs from the Gulf War.

It felt like another test when he first told her. He was flying to Helsinki the next day, and she wasn't invited. He was meeting with men higher up. He would have to drink twice as much as he wanted to and endure sitting around naked in a sauna then throwing himself in the icy lake. Back in the sauna he would have to match them joke for joke and laugh until his throat was scorched.

She is no idealist, she knows someone's got to do what he does. She just wasn't expecting it to be him. "How can you?" she blurted. His designs save lives, he said—protect innocent civilians during the necessary ordeal of war. "But you can't control how˙those things will be used." He stood there in front of her in shirtsleeves, collar unbuttoned, necktie loose, his weight slung over one foot, arms apart—another of his gestures, irresistible, ambiguous: *don't blame me, I guess I'm to blame, how about we take off our clothes?*

For that week he was away she practiced being without him, and it was flat—flat as the photographs of the wealthy she often paints from, flat as a student's drawing of an idea of the human form. Still she decided she was over him, she would end it when he got back. But then the phone rang and it was Marsh. "I think I love you," he said.

"How?" she asked. She has rather plain features and a body stronger on function than form—wide hips, muscular legs, breasts small enough not to sag. She'd been prepared to hang on to him tenaciously; she never figured that he might hang on back.

"You're not like most women. You don't make fusses, and you don't take forever getting ready." Then he added, "And you don't really need me." She might have been hoping for tenderness, yet had to admit here was someone who saw her exactly the way she wished to be seen.

"NOW we know where they get their revenue," Marsh mutters as they scan the menus at Cyril's. They will be lucky to get out for $150.

"Your first visit to the island?" asks the waiter. The dimness swallows his dinner jacket, the skin of his face, leaving the white plane of his shirt, the glint of his eyes. With meticulous gestures, he places two small napkins on the starched cloth and sets a drink in the center of each. "You must come back again."

"Don't worry, I'm not that hungry," she tells Marsh when the waiter leaves.

"Don't be ridiculous," Marsh says. "This is our honeymoon."

Around them in auras of candlelight she recognizes sun-burned faces from the flight out of San Juan. Beyond the window arches, the sky has faded to a pinkish gray and the water is dark as ink.

Marsh taps his bottle of beer against her drink, then lifts it to his lips with a spellbinding grace. Their honeymoon. All at once she feels shy—onstage with the curtain opening and no lines. They spent hours in the water today fighting the current, swimming out too far, to chunks of reef so deep they could see nothing but their own bluish, puny, frog-footed legs dangling down. Now hips thrust forward on his seat, shoulders and torso slouched, Marsh is talking about learning to scuba dive.

She sips her goblet of rum punch. "You know, you're not looking for fish," she says, "you're looking for trouble." He sits up straighter, raises his brows. "Danger," she answers. "If it doesn't feel dangerous, it isn't fun."

"Today wasn't dangerous," he says with a laugh—his credo, after all. "What was dangerous? You couldn't drown in this water if you tried."

"How about a barracuda bite?" Under the table she grabs at his thigh. Then he's trapped her wrist. "Well, take a tip from your wife, the artist," she says, as if his grip weren't too tight, "it's not in the flippers, it's in the eyes." She slurps her rum punch no-handed. "Are you happy we're married?"

"Of course," he says letting go.

"Aren't you going to ask me?" she says after a pause, but when dutifully he does, she laughs and says, "I hope that emerald green fish we keep seeing isn't on the menu. I'd hate to eat something that lovely, at least without realizing what I was doing."

"Let's do conch? They're ugly enough, the insides."

"I think my favorites were those little gold ones with the black and white spot on their bellies and the purple tails. How about you?" Marsh takes another swallow of beer. "Or maybe those fat black angel fish," she goes on, "trimmed with iridescent blue." He never stopped to notice any of them, she wants to rub it in—there were plenty of pretty fish close to shore.

Then he grins. "I vote for that snake, or whatever it was."

She refuses to react, holds her gaze on him, even, blank. What she can still see is the thick filigree of reef below them—reef like some sort of temple, arches behind arches, and mapping an inner corridor something sliding, long and gray. Once more she doesn't move or breathe for the eon that body eases under her, thick as an arm.

The waiter brings the extra spoons for their conch stew. Marsh leans back, hands clasped behind his head, as the young man aligns the new spoon with his knife, closes one eye then makes minute adjustments to the teaspoon and fork, until all four utensils are parallel and equidistant. The waiter is just as conscientious with hers. When he is gone, Marsh snatches up his clump of silverware and flings it back every which way onto the cloth. "What is it with that guy?" he says.

"He wanted to get it right. He thinks we care."

THE chief minister is pushing for independence; many on the island fear it, Mistress Crawford among them. They can make nothing grow in the sharp, cratered ground. They have no industry, they must bring everything in by boat. Their friendliness and their honesty have attracted tourists, but now there are rumors of gamblers, bad men trying to buy the beaches. "Nobody permitted to own beaches," she says. "It is island law." She repeats the quandary as though she knows it by heart: "If the British say dance, we got to dance."

She points to a sprawling two-story turquoise villa up the hill: the opposition leader lives there behind a chain-link fence. He knows how to seem to dance while doing other things, like turning sand into the concrete blocks which the new tourist hotels cannot be built without. Maybe she will vote for him in the election coming up. "But it don't make a difference which big man I vote for, he just get bigger, and the little people, they stay poor."

Marsh doesn't believe in impasse. Success is a matter of attitude, motivation, doing the job right. "Maybe if the little people would actually finish some of the construction around here," he says, "instead of sinking their money into a couple of walls and then giving up." He is trying to sound jovial, but the irritation creeps in. He can't get over all that reinforcing wire rusting along the rooflines like ornery hair. All those slabs of raw concrete losing their clean edge. And this inevitable woman, spoiling his bowl of Raisin Bran each morning, coming and going as if the villa were hers.

"It takes time, a house," Mistress Crawford says. "Islanders don't like to borrow money. Sometimes we wait two, three years for more money to come. Sometimes storms come so bad and we wait again two, three years. No one giving up."

THEY are heading back to the villa from a beach at the far end of the island. Marsh has been checking them off on his map as they explore their waters, one by one. Ana is raving as usual about the fish she has seen, this time the number of flounders: "You think you're looking at the bottom and then the light changes and you see one, all pastel speckles, and those two silly eyes."

Ahead in the dusty road a tall boy in a school uniform—pink shirt and maroon trousers—waves his thumb.

"Let's," she says, and with a sweep of her arm, gathers up all the towels and equipment in the back seat and piles them in her lap.

Marsh lurches to a gravelly stop. The boy gives a whistle, and three more dressed as he is come hurtling around the corner of a roofless structure of gray block—someone's investment, someone's gamble against time.

"My heavens," she says, with exaggerated chagrin. "How will you all squeeze in?" Laughing, they manage to. They all have perfectly shaped skulls, beautiful brows. She would have liked to sketch them, capture that spring in their bodies, all those dark, skinny arms.

They are going to the island harbor, the tall one says in a cracking voice. She points on the map to the villa where they are staying. "Your first time on the island?" he asks, showing her where to let them off. "Do you like friendly people?"

"Yes," she says. "Yes. Now when you see your road coming up, you yell STOP, OK?"

"OK," they say.

"It's a long way to the harbor," she says. "Isn't there a school bus you can ride?"

There is, but it is crowded. They would have to stand up.

"Not cool," she says.

"Not cool," they agree.

She asks them what time school starts and what time it lets

out; they each give a different answer, all at once. Then the tall one screams softly, politely, "Stop."

"Come back to our island," they say, almost in unison as they scramble out into the dust.

"Be nice to your mothers," she says back.

On the road again Marsh lets out a sigh. "I've been thinking," he says. "None of those fish you love can afford a portrait." He keeps staring ahead sternly. Ana isn't getting it. Then his head turns, he gives her a smirk. "There's no reason why you couldn't cut back on teaching and paint what you want to paint. I bet I could get the company to buy a couple of fish-and-coral scenes for the lobby. For starters. And if not, shoot, as far as I'm concerned, I make enough money for us both."

Her laugh feels a little shaky, hysterical. He is being considerate, she should be grateful, but instead she feels put on the spot, caught. As if she'd been engrossed in making a painting, and never realized somebody else was making one of her.

WHO else could this man be, towering over them in flowing purple silk at the entrance to the World's Famous Smitty's Very Native Bar and Grill, this man who bows, gathers up her hand, and kisses it, promising them the first drink free?

It is seven-fifteen and all the tables are empty. They accept a Caribe and a rum punch, but their responsibilities as sole guests keep Ana braced, nervous. As if somehow the whole picture might run together—woman behind the bar, waitress lighting globed candles with a tired Bic, TV on CNN, vases of fresh flowers, even imperial Smitty on the threshold, waving to passersby—all might simply decompose, without her steady approval.

After a while Smitty leaves his post and sweeps by their table, asks if they are happy. They assure him they are. "I go now to cook for you," he says and Ana nods gratefully as he disappears through a door in the back wall.

"He's got to make it such a big deal," Marsh grumbles. "This is a restaurant, for Pete's sake."

"It's probably good for business. Most tourists like to be fussed over."

"Friendliness as gross national product."

"They must feel terribly trapped, being dependent like this, always having to be nice? Mistress Crawford's right, whether it's the British or a bunch of tourists, or even racketeers, somebody else is always saying dance."

A MAN in a bowler hat, loose pants, and bright yellow silk shirt is playing "Eleanor Rigby" on the steel drum. A boy who has wandered into the restaurant, dressed in Michael Jordan's uniform right down to the sneakers, peers into its bowl, his eyes follow the man's swirling, rolling sticks. The man offers him one, but he shrinks from it with a shy smile. The rhythm shifts to salsa, inspirits the man's body, which revolves above his feet as the sticks revolve around the drum.

Others are finally wandering in also as Marsh and Ana begin to devour their platters of grilled crawfish—tourists whom Smitty comes out to fuss over, one group having invited their cab driver to have dinner with them. An island couple with a little girl listen to the music sipping Pepsi; two pasty, worn-looking women chat in British accents across the man sitting with them at the bar, skin like bitter chocolate. The waitress is busy instead of bored. Two girlfriends of hers have slipped into a table in the corner and are finding much to giggle about.

The air is redolent of grill smoke and garlic; the food, delicious. The steel drummer has begun to sing something about his island dream, while his instrument rings like a call to prayer. Shoulders sway, feet and hands tap, faces bob and smile. No one looks trapped; the springs of friendliness promise to bubble endlessly. Marsh lifts Ana's hand from the table, places it against his cheek, then kisses it. She is tempted to find Smitty and tell him—*everyone truly is happy now.*

"If I could only paint this." The words just come out.

"What this?" asks Marsh from behind her hand.

"This moment. This place. The World's Famous Smitty. And all these tourists mixing with the natives, or natives mixing with the tourists. No one having to try to be nice. And Mistress Crawford too. She's a beautiful subject. And all her J-daughters—I want to capture them too."

"I think they put too much rum in that drink," Marsh says.

"Because it can't last."

"You're right about that one," Marsh says, shifting his body around toward the wall. "Here comes trouble," he whispers, tipping his head toward three tall men who have materialized in the archway to outside, filling it up. The steel-drum player keeps wringing out his music, but voices lower a notch. Two of the men could be brothers, with their chiseled noses and jaws, hollows under their cheekbones so deep they look like slanting scars. They have on those hats that are really bags to hold their hair. Short dreadlocks tied into five knobs adorn the third one's skull. He has a flat nose and sad, sleepy eyes. He's the one who takes the first step into the room.

Each man has his walk, a special twist in the shoulders, hips, a bounce at the knees—it would be a miracle on canvas if caught, and Ana's sketch pad is still at the villa, still unpacked. Her desperate finger etches the air. Everyone is watching them, and they know it, these men who were boys not too long ago. They are proud to be seen.

As the leader approaches Ana's table, Marsh pulls his chair in, braces, actually closes his eyes. There is so much tension in his upper body that she can't help gasping when the first young man does put a hand on his arm. Marsh startles, flinches again when the other hand comes down on his shoulder, closing around it.

Marsh doesn't look up so he can't see what Ana knew seconds after she gasped, that this isn't trouble. The younger man gives Marsh a squeeze, then leans over to mumble something close to his ear—Ana hears the word *welcome,* the word *enjoy*—and then moves on.

Marsh's eyes glance around then lock on hers: did she see what just happened, all so fast, after all, and maybe if she didn't, he wouldn't have to react to it, do something, because it wouldn't count unless she saw it—waves of panic froth in his eyes then all at once recede. For a moment, it's as if something were washed away and he relaxes. He doesn't have to do anything. The young man is weaving among the tables greeting everyone the same.

HER brain feels pleasantly fuzzy with rum punch, salsa, and a desire that embraces all bodies, not only her husband's, though it is his specifically that she believed in, and it has somehow come through for her, not let her down.

They set out in their tiny Korean car to head back across the island, his hand on her thigh. She doesn't know how to bring up the man who touched him, yet she is filled with that man, him and his friends and Smitty and the drummer—they weren't trying to be friendly, they weren't trying to be anything.

"Maybe I *am* ready to take some time off," she tells Marsh. "To take painting seriously again." He nods and pats her leg. "What I'd really like is to come back here, maybe next fall, and bring all my stuff."

"The power of suggestion," Marsh says.

She shakes her head. "There are plenty of good reasons, actually, apart from all the grassroots PR." The night sky is a mess of stars, nothing remote about them, stars for the touching, light spills you could reach up and dabble in. The moon hangs crooked like a looped smile.

He's got both hands on the wheel. "It would be cheaper to buy a bunch of postcards."

"Well, fall's a long way off," she concedes. She doesn't want to break her mood with explanations, debate. They are coming into the central town—grocery store, bank, a couple of streetlights, the enclave of government buildings. Beyond them, just as the darker landscape resumes, their headlights spot some sort of problem— a line of vehicles stopped, half blocking the road, bodies milling around.

Marsh brakes still at a distance from it. They can hear the clamor of voices, urgency.

"An accident?" she says. "Maybe we can help." She reaches for her door handle. He grabs her other arm.

"I wouldn't do that," he says.

"That's OK." Her door is open. "I would."

He reaches across her and yanks it shut. "You may not leave this car," he says, staring ahead through the windshield at a man who approaches behind beckoning hands.

"I may not?" Another test? Or is he joking?

"For your own good," he says, and then the man is dancing toward her side.

Before Marsh can stop her, she's got her window rolled down.

"Freedom to the people," the man says.

"Yes, freedom. Absolutely," she says back.

"We're American tourists," Marsh barks out at the same time.

"Americans must join us," the man chants. "British go home."

She tries to concentrate on his words, ignore the smell of sour sweat. She hopes he will say more, so she can listen. If she is busy listening, she won't be afraid.

He calls something over his shoulder in the direction of the crowd then reaches through the open window and picks up her hand. She tries to pull it away but he won't let go, he is waving it, singing, "Americans must join us," then Marsh is leaning over her, leaning onto her, his elbow digs into her groin. He has shut the window on his side, locked his door, and now he punches the button down on hers and pumps her window up until it traps the man's arm. He gives the handle another turn. The man clutches her fingers tighter.

"Stop," she tries not to shout. "They're not going to hurt us. You're hurting him. And me. Stop."

Finally the man gives a howl and lets go, Marsh jerks the window down a notch then all the way up as soon as the arm is gone. But now there are more bodies breasting their headlights, bodies with excited faces, emitting undecipherable shouts.

"Now you've made them angry," she says.

Marsh throws the car in reverse, and it whines back away from the crowd. "We'll take another route," he says.

"All the way back to Smitty's then halfway around the island," she says dully, having got the tourist map by heart.

He is jerking the wheel like crazy, swinging the car into a three-point turn. In the middle of it, the running crowd reaches them, its faces loom at the windows, hands slap the roof.

There is a moment between reverse and forward. She has unlocked her door. She can feel what it would be like to plunge into the crowd, give herself over. The release.

The car lurches ahead. She is still inside it. "It may take hours," she says tonelessly. She's got her muscles braced against the heave of a fallen body under the tires.

"I don't care if it takes all night," Marsh pants through clenched teeth. "Any one of them could be packing a gun."

Any one of them gave the trunk two punches, a send off, then sealed tight, shoulder to shoulder, sucking in their own expelled breath, Ana and Marsh head back in the direction they came.

White

SAND tries to escape not because she thinks escape is possible, but in order to keep certain parts from going numb. She shrugs, flexes, twists, shifts her weight—unobtrusive protests against the binding of her hands behind her, to the bottom slat of one of her ladderback chairs. The wide front window of her cabin frames freedom—the undulant horizon dividing forested slopes, rock outcroppings, welts of golden grasses from a tooth-ache blue sky. *A view to die for,* she has thought. Now her heart stalls at the hyperbole, clutches its blood, then on the verge of bursting, releases it with a heavy throb.

Minutes ago she was outside, in broad daylight, bent almost double to pinch the unassuming blooms from her rows of basil, the purple-leafed, the lemon-scented, the ruffly. She sometimes talks to her crops, whispers apologies—this frustration of theirs is for the general good, she explains, it won't last forever, soon they'll be allowed to go to seed. She reminds them they have it pretty good in their beds of fluffy, conditioned soil, threaded with thin black hoses that drip, drip all morning. Outside the boxes only weeds with prickers and fat, furry leaves survive in the hard cracked earth.

Tending her basil has stretched and strengthened her, limbered her up, given her waistless, heavy-breasted body a taste of the dance, *pas de deux* with shovel or hoe. She can be her mother's daughter now that her mother is no longer capable of laughing at the comparison. Once upon a distant time, as doomed swan or consumptive courtesan, Velia died with sublime grace to awed sighs and applause. Now she is doing it for real, in undignified stages, demoted to the lowest level of a continuing-care facility, where she spends her days in a wheelchair, scrubbing the backs of her hands with her spit or trying to remove her socks.

Minutes ago, outside, in broad daylight, Sand had one of her panoramic visions—herself, enclosed by her patch of land, cradled by the valley, nestled in the mountains—and she had felt safe. She was a farmer now, she thought proudly, her uniform, the baggy white pants and white men's shirts she scavenged for next to nothing from the Salvation Army. White, to shield her from the scorching sun. White, the flag of rediscovered simplicity, fresh starts.

After spending most of her forty-nine years worrying herself sick, minutes ago she dared to think: *This must be how it feels not to have a worry in the world.*

Trudging up to the house for iced tea, she noticed the door was open. She stepped across the threshold, and startled at the sight of a stranger, standing at her sink, in her broad daylight, drinking her water from her glass. His hair was albino blond, straight and unkempt, his skin an unhealthy pink, and his eyes the color of bleached denim with tight little pupils. The blond stubble on his face caught the light and sparkled. He raised his other hand high enough for her to see its complicated grasp of a gun.

She leaned on the door frame, blinded for an instant, faint. *Hallucination*—her brain took a stab at reassurance—like the first time they tried her on Prozac and the dose was too high.

As if directing traffic, he waved her into her own house.

"I don't believe it," she said, but until recently, she always had, firmly believed in the omnipresence of disaster—if you didn't get hit by a car, or choke on a bite of meat, or develop a melanoma, then a lunatic might well break into your house. Parents, doctors, lovers mouthing probabilities couldn't shake her faith. No matter how gigantic the roulette wheel, the ball had to stop somewhere.

For reasons he didn't explain, this man had been trying to drive a truck along the railroad tracks. The tires had to give out somewhere. Hers was the nearest house. He spat a facetious, "Sorry." He wasn't shaving a spot beneath his lower lip, from which dangled a two-inch wisp of beard.

"Now, of all times," she said sadly. What a fool she'd been, lulled, tricked.

He looked at her, head cocked, until his eyes crossed.

"I'd stopped expecting you," she said.

He glanced around the cabin. "You expecting someone else? Husband? Kids? Cleaning lady?"

As if these were magic doors. Pick the right one and he would vanish. "My daughter."

He opened his mouth, closed it.

"Maybe my daughter. She didn't say for sure."

Through his teeth he said, "Don't do anything dumb, and you won't get hurt."

"You got that line from the movies," she said. Couldn't he see they were two halves of some statistic, pawns in a dreary game? Couldn't they change the rules?

"That's a dumb thing to say."

"I didn't mean you deliberately copied. You probably don't even realize—"

"Dumb."

"You're right. OK."

HER life arcs before her eyes like a joke on rainbows, a wobbly trail of fizzled careers, changes of address, ungentle men. Regular blasts of Velia's scorn to keep her expecting the worst so resolutely that the latest prescriptions never began to take the desperation away. Nor could Erica—child of still waters, born with unfathomable know-how—even Erica at her most diplomatic and dutiful could not completely calm her mother's fears.

Sand had wanted to work with her gifted hands, she kept thinking she could earn a living by contributing beauty to the world in the form of macramé, batik, necklaces and pierced earrings composed of feathers and beads. *Junk,* said Velia. *Wild goose chase. When are you going to get a real job?*

Sand didn't want to depend on any man. She was never caught by surprise when they left her. Alone again, she and Erica repossessed the queen-sized bed, picnicked there on pizza and popcorn, played Old Maid, and watched TV. Sand plugged back in the nightlight and dozed off with her eyes fixed on it: if its glow suddenly went dark, she'd know an intruder, possibly lunatic, had passed over the threshold, and her plan was always to push Erica off the bed on the side next to the wall, then roll underneath it after her. Sometimes she slept with an extra pillow across her chest to blunt the force of a bullet or knife.

Maybe all those men had been intruders, somewhat lunatic, she thinks now. The last of them, Rob, moved with her into this valley, then used her credit card to buy a sea kayak and take off for Alaska. He needed more action, he said. "You belong here, you're a gatherer. I'm still into the hunt."

One of the first, Erica's father, would never have known his daughter existed until Erica started asking questions, begging for his name. *What did you do to make him go? Couldn't you have hung onto him for my sake? Am I like him?*

No, not at all, Sand told her, not intending to lie. He had receding hair, after all, acne scars, and big, bumpy knees. Whereas Erica was peaches-and-cream perfect, she played soccer like a dancer, she was a miracle Sand couldn't understand, probably hadn't deserved. But like her father, Erica was mainstream, savvy and deep-down hard-hearted—prom queen from the word go. Ninety-nine chances in a hundred father and daughter would click when they finally met. Sure enough, Erica went.

When Sand and success finally clicked, she was painting fingernails. She rose from an hourly wage in a shopping mall to her own burgeoning business, a boutique and adjunct school offering eight-week training courses to would-be nail artists. In certain circles she became famous for her fine, single-bristle renditions of ballerinas, each finger performing a different move—pirouette, jeté, chassé, coupé—and an arabesque across the diagonal of each thumb.

The year before she cashed it all in to buy her farm, she went to Houston for the annual conference and competition of the National Association of Nail Artists, and took home the $10,000 award for first place.

Success felt hollow. The art of fingernails had proven repetitive, mechanical, commercialized. As a career, it had gelled too late. Too late to keep Erica from moving in with her hero of a father, who bought her a Honda and promised to send her to Stanford.

When Sand called Velia with news of her prize, Velia said, "Delicious apples are fine as long as they're crisp, but once they start getting mushy, I don't want them."

HE asked for a hammer. "Don't try anything," he said. As if she were thinking up strategies. Instead of not thinking scary thoughts. Different parts of her body trembled when called upon, but her mind she swept root-canal blank, made it cling to an old mantra: *just do what you're told, by this time tomorrow it will be over.*

Yes, but.

It won't kill you.

No?

He wasn't impressed with the loose-headed tool she produced from the pantry, or with the flower pot of bent rusty nails she had collected digging the beds for her herbs and never gotten around to throwing away.

He nodded toward a set of louvre doors. "That the only closet?" He didn't like having to ask her things, having to wait for answers. He would have liked to barge around checking for himself. Minutes ticked by of his shallow breathing, his face stretched into a pastel grimace. The miniature beard hung from his lower lip like a single bucktooth. He had on camouflage pants whose earth tones had faded from countless washings and heavy-soled combat boots.

His bright white shirt was from The Gap. One hand wore that gun her eyes must avoid, the other clutched a broken hammer and a terra-cotta pot. Maybe he always looked like that—wildly impatient, almost alarmed. Erica's age. A kid out of control.

He didn't like having to follow her. "Who in the fuck built this house anyway?" He stopped short in her bedroom, turned on her.

"I don't know," she said. "I haven't lived here that long."

"You'd think they'd of put in one decent closet." He lifted a boot and kicked at one of the louvre doors to the walk-in. "Piece of shit," he said. "How'm I supposed to nail these suckers shut?"

"I don't like them either. They're on my list to replace. Do you know how much a solid door runs? I haven't made any profit yet, and closing costs wiped out my—"

"Lady, shut up."

She thought she heard fear mixed with anger—thought she glimpsed a human being behind the mask. "I'm not trying to make you feel guilty. Things'll work out eventually. I don't have much here but you're welcome to anything—"

He hurled the pot of nails at the corner of the room, it landed with a clank and broke into large pieces. So did her empty poise. She clenched her chattering teeth. "If I can't nail you in a closet, how am I supposed to keep you out of the way?"

His question triggered echoes. She thought she saw her panic flicker behind his pale eyes.

"I can stay out of the way," she said, without expression, forced to the script.

He motioned her back out to the great room.

"That's one thing I'm good at." She was talking to herself. "It's why I'm here."

"You got any rope?"

"Rope?"

"Rope, lady." He danced his weight from one boot to the other, then back. "Jesus Christ, do you think I've got all day?"

"I'm just trying to think. There's a ball of twine I used—"

His free hand had yanked a knife from the wooden block next to the sink; now while the hand with the gun pinned the phone cord against the counter, he chunked the blade down so hard that odd noises escaped her lips. He looked pleased, proud of the sounds. He came toward her with a long corkscrew of cord, backed her into the chair. He smelled like the summer muck exposed by the receding water of her pond.

He let go of the gun, she could feel it there, by her feet. "It's for your own good," he told her in a different voice. He fumbled with her hands, the cord—his touch was rough, angry that she was old enough to be his mother. "In case there's a shoot-out," he said.

Another spurt of fear, but feebler now, despite the vision—her trapped in this chair, a sitting duck, bullets shattering windows, ricocheting off walls, friendly, deadly fire.

"In case they bring in a SWAT team, you know. They want me bad."

OUTSIDE, above the mountains' infinite regress she sees her mother dancing, a lone cloud of white tulle, white flashes of satin shoe. She hears her mother's voice—ever confident that it is addressing a matter of universal concern: "The whole business of bearing down goes against everything I have trained my body to do; in ballet, you see, you must be weightless, you are always willing yourself up, into the air, to hang there for that impossible extra second, so you see how difficult it is, childbirth, the damage to a dancer's instinct, her spirit really, you see?"

Sand's brother had just been born, he was waking in the middle of the night crying. Four-year-old Sand knew why. In the sound of his cry she saw gaping space, a giant empty sleeve. Her family teetered like made-in-Japan dolls on its brink.

No one had sat her down and said, Sand, the Russians have the Big One now, and it would be a year still until she started kindergarten and learned how to march single file into the cloakroom, there to fold herself into a fetal mound, hands clasped around the back of her head. And there were many years ahead of lurking, all-natural dangers—leukemia, lockjaw, quicksand, lightning, tuna fish contaminated with botulism, and Velia's favorite: splinters that entered your bloodstream and wasted your heart. Many years, and then Sand's own father, Air Force Ace, would begin dropping little ones on the people of Hanoi, and they, placing no value on human life, would finally shoot him out of the sky.

Yet it was as if all these possibilities were released by her new brother's inconsolable wailing, they careened around in her brain until she had to cry out in the night herself, dragging her exhausted mother out of bed once again—to warn everyone, to get them to do something, if anything could be done.

What the just-retired ballerina and just-promoted jet pilot did was sigh one more time at the nuisance Sand could be, but they zipped her into her snowsuit, wrapped up the future Commander-in-Chief of the Armed Forces in his baby blankets, and carted the whole family over to the base hospital emergency room—just in case it was her appendix. The doctor, her parents, everyone got mad at her when it wasn't.

"I never said anything about a stomach ache," she tells the farthest misty ridge. "That was their idea." The ache had come from someplace else, which had just caught the truth of forever and alone.

HE is in her bathroom, taking a shower, taking his time. Using her shampoo and her soap. The water stops. His voice rings through her two rooms: "You got an extra toothbrush?"

She clears her throat but her answer falters, drops in her lap.

"Hey, lady, I gotta have something to brush my teeth with."

She collects her breath, forces out, "The only toothbrush I have is my own."

"It's mine now," he calls back.

"You're welcome," she says softly, in the tone she used to use to remind Erica, who is her father's now. She has seen her daughter only once since the night she, Sand, got home from her shift at the video store to a dark apartment, nothing cooking, and then the sheet of paper torn from a spiral notebook, the bulgy, slightly back-slanting script, "I've decided to go stay with my dad for a while. Please don't try to call me for six months. I've decided I have a right to a stable, normal life. Also don't expect an answer if you write." The i's were dotted with hearts.

The surrender of a toothbrush is nothing after that.

| | |

VELIA, svelte in black and high, high heels, crosses her ankles, raises her long, boneless fingers to her throat, and decides to tell the truth. In an opposite corner slouches a vague recollection of Sand's first psychiatrist, who thought it might be useful to get Velia's input, before he decided why lumpy Sand at Erica's age couldn't decide anything at all.

For example, what to wear to school? What if she chose her cotton jumper and it wasn't warm enough and she caught a cold which turned into pneumonia and she died? But what if her woolen one with the full skirt got caught in the closing door of the bus when she got off? Then she'd be yanked off her feet and dragged along the street receiving enough lacerations and contusions to cause her to die. No choice was death-free. Nothing for it but go back to bed.

"Cassandra has always been difficult," Velia says. "Scared of her own shadow. Withdrawn. I suppose I've never understood, since when I was her age all I wanted to do was perform, meet new people, travel the world. Her father too"—she touches her hanky to the inside corners of her eyes—"was a charming daredevil. Do you know what I think the problem might be?" The shrink doesn't, but Sand knows what her mother will say.

Nothing about Sand's love for her father, now missing in action, her complete devotion to him in spite of the mix of criticism and neglect she got in return. Nothing about how more and more Sand's girlbody is also missing under layers of belly and breast.

"I hate to say this," Velia says, but she doesn't really. She always loved it when the truth hurt. "Richard and I never planned on a family. I was a dancer, the sky was the limit, Christensen as much as promised me my day would come. Except Cassandra came first, a complete accident. The beginning of the end of my career."

HIS bare footfalls thud heavy behind her. Though her nerves cringe, she doesn't let herself move. Then a hand grabs the back of her neck and, as she gasps, releases it with a shove.

He barrels across her vision dressed in only his pants and the illusion of a tank top where his sunburn stops. He still clutches the gun. He darts his head around the front window then ducks away. His back is pale as unbaked bread but well-muscled, V-shaped. It's the shape she always pictured as she rubbed the flabbier, scrawnier backs that found their way into her bed. Water beads along the valley of his spine.

You'd think a body like that must contain some vein of goodness.

He has flattened his perfect torso against the wall beside a side window. He is looking for a fight.

He moves in abrupt jerks, one minute here, the next there, and all she can do is wait to find out which story the separate moments will cohere to create.

Which headline?

What do they want him for?

She bars the possibilities from her mind. The important thing is to keep flexing the numbness out of her hands and wrists.

"Anything out there?" She tries to sound matter-of-fact, neutral.

"You can't never tell," he says.

"I don't think this county has a SWAT team," she says.

"It's got nothing to do with this county." His eyes are on her— they cross and he blinks them straight.

She doesn't ask what it does have to do with.

"Where's your TV?"

"I don't own one." No TV anymore, no tasseled pillows, no dried flowers and eucalyptus, no brass elephants, no paisley table scarves, no Matisse posters, no decorator's fishnet, no strings of little white lights. No mother, no daughter. No stash of Xanax and Zoloft for when her moat of anxiety floods its banks. No toothbrush. Suddenly that seems the definitive loss.

"You had a TV, you'd know who I am. You wouldn't be sitting there wondering was I one of those crazies, running around killing for the thrill of it."

As opposed to? She doesn't ask.

"They're waving around this attempted murder thing cause I

punched out a Mexican south of Red Bluff and he cracked his head on the way down. Fucking insult," he says, drawing himself up to attention. "If I'd of been attempting, that cucaracha would of been dead." His lips stretch in a smile, to reveal flecks of decay—poor toothbrush, infected forever. "The government gets you coming and going, don't it?"

She drops her head—half a nod.

He uses her hair to pull it up again. "Lady, I'm asking you a question."

"Accidents happen," she says hoarsely.

"OK. And I'm telling you there's plenty would like to do what I do, if they'd got the balls for it. Trouble with this country, nobody does anymore. Guys keep handing them over to you ladies. Know what I mean?"

She doesn't try to muffle her sigh, deep as a sob: in over your head, the drawing of the breath you know will drown you.

"Say something, damn it."

"I'm thirsty," she says.

The machine he is shifts into a different gear. "Sorry, my fault." He stomps over to the sink to fill her coffee mug with water, then stomps back to where she sits. He bumps the mug against her teeth and water spills down her shirt. He sets the gun on the table and tries again, grabbing the back of her head in one hand, guiding the mug with the other. As fast as she swallows, water still runs down her chin, soaking her collar.

He doesn't notice. "Whose balls you got buried out there in that garden of yours?"

The rim of the mug between her teeth, water pouring into her.

"Don't look so scared, it was a joke." He grabs a dishtowel and scrubs clumsily at the front of her shirt. "Bet you must of won a few T-shirt contests in your day." He swoops over to a window again. "I'm more into legs myself."

He heads back to the bedroom. "Holler if you see anything," he tells her. "It's for your own good."

What did it mean, *good*, or for that matter, *her own*? She has not led the life she pictured for herself—she's always thought she would do something original and world-shaking—world-helping: something that would change everyone's mind about her. She always thought she still had time.

"TELL me about that car out there," he calls from the other room.

A burst of hope, unexpected and breathtaking as a kick in the chest.

"You gotta talk up," he calls.

She clears the *if only's* from her throat, the deals she is ready to make in exchange for one last chance. "It's ten years old. It has about 90,000 miles."

"I can see that." He is in front of her again, fully dressed. "How does it run?"

"I haven't had any problems. I wouldn't try it over railroad tracks though."

He looks at her blankly, cross eyed, then grins an insincere "Ha ha," and gives her cheek a couple of I-get-it slaps.

"You've got almost a full tank of gas. You ought to be fine."

"I do, do I? What about you?"

"Me?"

"What're you going to do the next time you get thirsty up here all alone? How're you going to take a leak with this chair tied to your back."

Matter-of-fact, neutral. "You could untie me."

"What I could do is take you with me."

His words slice right to the nerve holding her together. Tears spring to her eyes. "Please," she says. "Leave me here."

"You're just what I need, a juicy bargaining chip. Hey, how do you think it makes me feel when you do that?"

Through a film she sees the cabin empty, swaddled in spider webs, the basil beds choked by the explosive seeds of thistle, wild rose, mullein. She is mourning her lives, the ones she imagined, the ones she got.

At least she's been allowed to go to seed.

Maybe that's all there is, maybe the rest—beauty, romance, peace, and the general good—is nothing, society's PR.

At the kitchen counter he is throwing open cabinet doors, rum-maging.

"I have a daughter," she says.

"She have nice legs?" He sets aside a box of microwave pop-corn, a bag of granola. "I take it you're too good for junk food."

"I need to write my daughter a note. Explaining."

"What's to explain? Man, I'd give my shirt about now for a half-dozen jelly doughnuts. Wanna know how I like to eat them?"

"You are not her fault."

He stops, steps away from the kitchen so he can look at her, eyes the color of dirty ice. He shakes his head. "Dumb."

"I don't want her to feel guilty for the rest of her life. Thinking there's something she should have done."

His dazed irises slide toward his nose. "What?"

"She needs to know I forgive her for not forgiving me." For graduating from high school two hundred miles away then coming back and rounding up two old soccer teammates to help her load the contents of her room into the Blazer she borrowed from her dad. Shelves of perfectly preserved Barbie dolls and unicorns and trophies, posters of Madonna and Tom Cruise. "She needs to know I don't forgive myself," Sand added, for being afraid to protest as all remaining evidence of Erica disappeared into black plastic bags.

She could have tried harder, promised to change, thrown her-self in front of the Blazer's wheels. Instead she'd acted as though she'd approved of the plan.

"Excuse me, but you sound like a couple of nut cases." He gives up on foraging, slams each cabinet door so hard it flies back open.

To each loud crack she thinks *no*. Erica is not a nut case. Velia, yes, Sand, maybe. But Erica wasn't, must never be. "In the event that something happens to me." There.

He relaxes, beams. "Something already has. If you'd of had a TV, maybe you'd be showing a little respect."

She has gone too far to retract. "Something worse." The words may fend the something off, they may pave its way.

He is back in his element. "What do you think could be worse?"

She refuses to say.

"I wish to hell you'd answer my questions."

"My hands have gone to sleep, I've got cramps in both arms, I don't know."

"The point is I can do what I want."

"If that's a question, yes. You could let me write a note to my daughter."

"No time," he says, abruptly preoccupied with the concealed sharpshooters he imagines outside. "We gotta load some of this stuff into the car and then we're outta here."

"I do need to use the bathroom."

"Shit." He throws up his arms, gun and all. His eyes go blank, he breathes faster—he is trying to think.

She watches his face, sees the moment when a team of he-men with telescopic rifles melts into an old woman peeing all over the seat of a car.

He unties her hands as if they are cabinet doors; luckily they are beyond feeling.

"Don't do anything dumb," he grumbles, as if he knows he's repeating himself. He gives the gun a flourish. "If I hear anything I'm not supposed to hear—I'm standing right outside."

HER hands have been retied but more loosely. She has been loaded into the passenger side of her car, a sack of provisions plopped on her lap. Along the seam of the grocery bag, she reads the information *Made with pride by Victor Morales.* More PR, she thinks. The gun rides the middle seat, in plenty of space.

He swings onto her long driveway, swerves with it around the old madrone tree with its two trunks—the original upright one dead and gray, the other rich red one pushing out at an angle, almost as thick.

He slows for the sharp turn onto the dirt and gravel road down from her cabin, which will take them to the paved road, an old highway, which in either direction leads to the interstate.

As quail scurry for cover in the blackberry hedges, she can see them coming, in broad daylight, the seven houses below hers. Seven chances for someone to block their momentum, for something improbable to happen, change the story, break the rules. In a year, she has rarely glimpsed any of these possible someones, much less met them. Like her, they know how to stay out of the way.

There is the house with the sheep and miniature goats; across from it, the A-frame you can only discern in winter. Then the low, gray contemporary sits in the middle of its cleared field of yellow grass, and on the other side of the road, the sprawling two-story faces the other way, displaying its terraced back garden of orange lilies and lavender.

In the rear view, these things disappear along with her basil farm, behind a cloud of dust.

Ranks of blue chicory and Queen Anne's lace point forward, to the clear, sharp strip of macadam at the base of the hill. Near the corner, the bright white wad of a soiled Pamper tossed from a car days ago, which she and her neighbors have decided to ignore.

A jet trail melts into the wild blue. There is no hope of a cloud. Yet in the silence blooming like a heavy odor, someone is about to arrive, her portal shrunk to a single point in space, in time.

The car doors don't lock. Sand can work both hands behind her around to her right, until her fingers touch the handle, pry it out. The door swings open with a loud crank, she tucks her head and rolls.

He is driving too fast, though not fast enough.

Her brain shrivels in the pain that flares along her right side, she is nothing but burning arm. In some mind other than hers, the car's skid registers. It slides forever, gravel sputtering, dust belching, until it finally stops.

With the fight that comes to people in emergencies, she works herself onto her knees, plants one foot in the dirt, but cannot rise. Victor Morales's bag has flown off into the blackberries. Her white clothes are covered with dirt and dust.

She tries to scream, and finds her mouth full of dust.

Seeking something wet, her tongue tastes blood.

"Help," she calls, but her voice is a whisper, her right arm much too loud. "Please, everyone, anyone, help."

In some mind other than hers, the wheels spin, catch and spin, and the car is in motion again, slow motion, backing up the hill. Some other mind sees a fleck of white stuck in the road, fluttering, a final flag.

She pushes the one foot as hard as she can against the earth, she lifts her weight into a stand. "I want you to forget this. Things like this don't happen," she says, willing her feet from one step to the next. "I'm all right, see? Not really hurt." She is sure she is making progress, eyes on her plot of land. "The important thing is you're here. Finally. And we can get on with the rest of our lives."

Affairs of Strangers

*T*HE first night I have trouble with the man's face. It isn't handsome or even striking, but the angle is tricky, somewhere between a three-quarter view and a straight profile. I can't bring myself to bear down on the pencil. After fifteen minutes the spray of lines on my tablet is still so faint that the instructor comes over, sort of sniffs at the paper, and says, "You begin by making mistakes. You make enough mistakes and you find a truth in them. Notice the tension in that shoulder."

When I look at the man posed on the stool in our midst, I see a black ribbed turtleneck and gray flared pants, I see boot heels hooked over a bottom rung. His left fist is planted at his waist and his right arm rests on his right thigh. Its long dark fingers hang down between his spread knees. "I have always liked doing faces," I tell the instructor. "I did my husband's three grandchildren from school photographs and gave them to him for Christmas the year he died." The instructor is a young man with the cheeks of a cherub and a diabolic goatee. He purses his mouth and stretches his eyes wide. I have said more than I should have. He bows his head and moves on.

There is one other older student across the room. Every few minutes, his furtive eyes and neatly combed gray hair appear to the left of his easel, along with one pale hand, pencil poised like a teacup, then he disappears again behind it. Later when we tape our papers up on one wall, I will see that he has captured the man in the hard concise lines of a cartoon. He is the only one of us who adds background—a Roman ruin of broken columns.

By the end of the hour I have mostly face, dark-skinned face and knitted cap pulled down over ears to their large gummy lobes. Gaunt cheeks, nose that hardly dents at the bridge, heavy lips, long but unaggressive chin. A gentle horsey face balanced on a vague body with impossibly lopsided legs. The instructor tugs at his beard and calls my effort impressionistic.

Then he praises the drawing of the girl who worked next to me at the easel which caught the man head on. Her hair hangs in uncombed tendrils, and she has the wild, damp look of a child whose fever has just broken. When she wasn't tromping out into the hall to smoke cigarettes, she held a wedge of charcoal sideways and blackened her paper with stormy loops and strokes. The instructor calls attention to her composition. The body is so huge it is headless and runs off the edge of the sheet on one side. The instructor talks about the central negative space between the remaining arm and the body and also between the legs. She has got the tension in the left shoulder.

The man himself stands outside the arc of us along the wall. Arms crossed over his chest, he studies what we have done with him and it seems to make him sad. I begin to wish I had made him more handsome, but then I realize, No, that is not what I am here for. Whatever my reason is, it's not that.

MY sister likes to call to berate me for never calling her. "I can't let you get away with this," she tells me. When I ask her what *this* is, her voice stiffens with familiar authority. "Withdrawing from life," she says.

Even though I got through this Christmas without a twinge,

I tell her I am still grieving. "You're supposed to grieve when you lose your husband," I say. For weeks I made a fetish of his dirty laundry, gathered the body-softened clothes in my arms, took long whiffs of them and wept. But as their pungency faded, so did the pain, a surprise compared to the anguish of two divorces.

Lately I have been packing away photographs—vacations at Myrtle Beach, Hugh and I moderately lumpy in our bathing suits, squinting into the sun, waving; Thanksgiving with his dutiful children, pointing in polite awe at the turkey—pleasant, meaningless times I am ready to put behind me. I have been trying to sort through Hugh's files—taxes, bank statements, car repairs, warranties on all those things he decided we owed ourselves, the food processor, the trash compactor, the device that opens the garage door by remote control. Fifteen years of marriage reasonably organized and warrantied, as though everything did not eventually fall apart.

A clever invention, marriage, something you are taught to imagine you need. I suspected it when I left my first husband; should have known by the time I left my second. I will never admit this to my sister—she would too heartily agree. I say, "I just haven't felt like doing anything."

"That's depression," she says. "You've got to make a list every morning and then do what it says."

"Maybe I've done everything I care to do," I tell her, knowing that she has never given me credit for doing anything. Anything would have been following her to Frostburg State for a teaching degree, not putting the boy I loved through college and giving birth to his son, when no one thought he had it in him. After that, anything was designing New Math curriculum, not being a mere office manager and designing the first brochure for what is now the largest plastic surgery practice in the Washington area. Anything could never mean marrying one of the doctors or having his daughter or staying home with the two children and making everything from scratch. Or breaking the habit of drinking a little too much. After ten years the house had gotten too big; there were always people in it I didn't recognize—carpenters, accountants, cleaning women, kids on the verge of adolescence. My own children couldn't hide their impatience with me, like professional actors stuck with an absent-minded amateur. For my fortieth birthday, that husband made me an appointment with his partner for the new miracle fanny tuck.

"If I could start over with Sam and Sarah, I would," I tell my sister now. We have had family therapy in several combinations, and maybe one of these days, as my children face middle age, they will stop trying to punish me by hurting themselves. They both stick to the West Coast and change addresses often.

"You shouldn't dwell on them," she says, "it will only depress you more." She suggests the galleries, the Kennedy Center, she offers to initiate me into the mysteries of duplicate bridge. She invites me to swim as a guest at her community indoor pool, where she logs a mile every other day, at the same time composing a sonnet in her head.

A couple of weeks ago she pinned me down to lunch in the Pavilion, the center of this community called Leisurama, which excludes the younger generations by means of a six-foot wrought-iron fence and round-the-clock guards. After thirty-seven years of teaching high school algebra, my sister retired and bought one of the first condos there. It has more than doubled in value. In the cafeteria, she settled us next to the dazzling mural of tropical birds and told me she had the solution to everything—a two bedroom with den opening up downstairs from her. "You and I are going to buy it together," she said.

"What for?" I assumed she was broaching an investment scheme.

"To live in, silly. The two of us." She pauses and pats at her perfect French twist. "You always have to make it hard for me, don't you?"

"We can't do that," I said.

"Surely, you're not expecting to get married *again?*"

"We'd never get along." I am surprised that she has forgotten this.

"It overlooks the golf course. With two bathrooms. That house of yours is nothing but a burden."

"I could never live here," I said. She put down her fork and pinched one eyebrow into a frown. I try to laugh. "You look just like Mother," I said.

"Believe me, I can appreciate what she went through with you."

"I'm sixty years old, for heaven's sake. You don't have to take care of me."

"I'm not getting down on my knees," she said. "The apartment is lovely and you won't see a blade of crabgrass or a speck of trash anywhere. There's the underground mall for shopping. Life is safe and utterly comfortable. At our age, we deserve that."

"I don't know," I said, swayed for a moment by her conviction. "Everything is so . . . finished."

She raised a finger and shook her head. Her eyes twinkled. "Even as we speak, they're making improvements—digging tunnels under us, putting in moving sidewalks to connect every building to the mall. In bad weather you'll never have to go outside."

It surprised us both when tears came to my eyes. "I like going outside," I said. "I don't want to be stuck in some tunnel. Why won't you leave me alone?" I took my glasses off and wiped them on a napkin.

When my sister tried to reach across and pat my hand, she knocked a vase with a fern and a mauve rose onto the mauve and green carpet. Luckily the flora were silk. "I'm sorry," she said, straightening the wire stems.

"It wouldn't fit in with my plans," I said gently.

"What plans? You never have any plans." Her voice thinned to a shriek. "You don't care about anything. You're letting yourself go. You're going to turn into a crazy old woman."

My sister doesn't usually get upset like that, and it scared me. "I've decided to go back to school," I said.

SHE is right about the house being a burden. It was eighty years old when Hugh and I bought it, and it misses his bursts of care. The drains are temperamental, the ceilings have blistered from leaky, inaccessible pipes. Hugh never really figured out the wiring—lights go through phases of flickering, circuits break for no reason, and in corners of the basement, bulbs hang from sockets whose switches are not to be found.

Sometimes I dream that I am living in a bare room in a strange bright city, whose language I can speak fluently as long as I never stop to think. Awake, I have wondered about monasteries and convents, and whether encased in such simple discipline something stubborn in me might finally give. But my sister was the disciplined one, the good one; I was difficult, self-centered. I think I have always been looking for something that wasn't there.

On the second night of my art course, the man wears only a cotton pouch between his legs. We have stationed ourselves around the half circle of easels and he comes out of a sort of storeroom that no one saw him enter, and takes off a dingy short coat of fake sheepskin, and leans against the back wall, ankles crossed, as if he were all dressed up on a street corner waiting to meet someone. The pouch glares white against his brown body. A noise like sea roar fills my head and I feel deeply alone.

The instructor is calling for a series of five-minute studies. I order myself to raise my charcoal, make a mark on the paper, try to do what everyone else is doing, scribbling vigorously, ripping off pages, scribbling again. The instructor is standing somewhere behind me, urging, "Realize the movement, the physical impulse, not the position." Is he talking to me or that fierce-eyed girl with the messy hair beside me? "Feel it in your own body," he says before he moves on. I start to perspire from the effort.

The man is much older without his clothes and cap. His hair is short and gray, and arthritis has swollen one knee to an awful size. My eyes can't resist that knee; my own knees start to ache. If only the stroke of charcoal on paper could give some consolation. My drawings get larger as I imagine the skin peeled away and my hand discovering tendons, dark swirls of kneecap, knots of cartilage. I press them onto the paper, black on black, like proof of injustice. The instructor comes around again, and groans softly. I'm sure it is me he is disappointed in. When we take a break and tape our drawings on the wall, there are a lot of men without any knees to speak of, and then my knees without men.

"Obsession is the essence of gesture," the instructor says when he gets to my sketches. "A craving for the thing itself, and not some fixed symbol of the thing." The words make me flush with confusion. Everyone turns my way, trying to figure out whether I have been praised or reproved, whether they should pay more attention to knees in the future or less. Everyone except that one girl, who keeps scanning the row of drawings, back and forth. Her own figures are small this time, crowded onto the page, wrestling with themselves. "Pregnant with what's about to happen," the instructor says. Her eyes dart to mine with a harried look.

The naked man himself rests in a crooked adirondack chair in the corner, his old coat thrown over his shoulders, his bad knee, a huge hairless globe, crossed over his good. He has put on half-glasses and appears to be reading his mail.

At six-thirty, when class is over, I am reluctant to leave the bright warmth of the studio. I have on my poncho, I have wrapped my muffler around my head and neck, my tablet is under one arm, a treasury of knees and the bodies that finally began to grow from them, strange hieroglyphics. It's as if I'm forgetting something in the clutter of easels, stools, old chairs, leaning shelves and stained tables piled with pine cones, shriveled fruit, wooden blocks and balls, empty tin cans, bottles, a conch shell, hunks of grubby cloth, and fraying baskets. I am the only one left besides the instructor. I wish he would say something to me, it doesn't matter how conventional. He smiles around the unlit cigarette in his mouth and zips up his backpack. "Hey Victor," he calls to the empty room. "Catch the lights and lock up before you leave." Then he disappears. Then the door to the storeroom opens, and the man himself comes out in his cap and sweater and pants again, shrugging his coat on straight. He nods to me. I don't move. Bowed over his own fingers buttoning, he asks me, "Do I *look* dead?"

I can't speak.

"Damn Social Security folks keep mailing me letters informing me that I am dead." With a flourish of one dark hand, so slow and graceful it seems to mock my fear, he ushers me out of the room ahead of him.

"That's absurd," I say.

He gazes down at me through half closed eyes, long, straight lashes and nods. "I wrote and told them," he says.

"How are you supposed to receive a letter if you're dead, much less read it and answer it?"

"Guess those lazy-ass bureaucrats believe in ghosts," he says.

Outside it feels like snow. He is heading in one direction, to the bus stop; I, in the other, to the parking lot. He pats my shoulder. "Don't you go wasting any pity on that knee of mine," he says. "Most days, I don't even know it's there."

AT the beginning of our next class, the instructor makes a big production out of plugging in a space heater and setting it on the corner of the model's platform against the wall. When the coils have begun to glow red, Victor appears from the storeroom, the coat comes off, and he is naked. I am the one who feels exposed, as if the instructor must know I'm not ready for this, may never be. It is not the nudity—I have had three husbands, there have been lovers. It's that Victor is a stranger, we are all strangers. And he doesn't do anything but stand there, inviting us to look.

My arm attacks the tablet with resentful smears, each one demanding, *Is this necessary? Is this really necessary?* I am so determined not to avoid the genitals that I render them in more detail than anything else. When I step back I am horrified at the way they stand out, dark and dense with spite.

The instructor smirks with pleasure. He holds up the tablet that belongs to the fierce girl, whose name is Dana, and waves his free hand over its black snarls. "Mass is the revelation of energy," he says. "Build it out like this from the body's core. Follow it back to where every posture, every tip of the head, every turn of the ankle begins." Dana twists a piece of hair around and around one finger and glares at her boots. The others nod their earnest faces.

Its eyes blank as an ancient statue's, Victor's body reveals itself in three-minute postures—tired, belligerent, nonchalant, pensive, mournful—each ending when the instructor calls out, "Change."

I can't wait to get out of there. I leave the building behind

Dana, who immediately lights a cigarette. I have to skip every other step to keep up with her. She explains that she has to get home, because it's her turn to help fix dinner for her housemates, and home is a three-mile hike. Her voice is hoarse. She is wearing only a men's undershirt and leather vest under her jean jacket. I offer to drive her. "No pay backs?" she says, tossing her wild hair.

"No smoking in the car," I tell her.

"No problem," she says.

On the road, I say, "You draw with such confidence. I wish I could."

"You want to know my trick?" she asks. "Don't care, don't think, just do it."

"Maybe I'd be better off with a different model."

"Don't care," Dana says again. "That's how it works."

"Maybe next week they'll give us someone else."

"If you're hoping for good looking guys and stuff, don't hold your breath," she says.

"I don't know what I'm hoping for," I say.

"I took the course before for a couple of weeks and all we got to draw were two anorexic chicks and this guy with a dick the size of my big toe."

"How do you mean, you took the course before?"

"That teacher was this total weirdo. We had a personality conflict and stuff."

She directs me down a side street to a stop at the bottom of the hill. Tucked among the brick colonials is an older bungalow with overgrown shrubbery. The bare bulb over the front door reveals a porch clogged with furniture and a couple of trash cans. An invisible dog starts barking.

"What are you having for supper?" There is something else I want to know; I am stalling until I can think of what it is.

"The usual," she says. "Tacos." She explains, "It's the only thing anyone knows how to make."

"How many of you live here?" I ask.

"Of us?" She fiddles vaguely with her mittened hands. "A bunch." She forces a grin. "The neighbors hate us. I mean they

want us to have a place to live and stuff, but not on their street."
Her pronouns pulse with the unfairness. I do not ask anything else.
She gathers up tablet and satchel and jerks open the door. Then
she tells me, "My mother thinks it's perverted to take off your
clothes."

"I wonder what that makes us who draw it."

"Damned to hell," she says.

THE temperature has dropped another ten degrees. It is too cold
for snow; it is too cold for me to leave the house for a silly class I
never should have signed up for. What *was* I hoping, to be the next
Grandma Moses? To prove to the world some hidden talent, my
undiscovered worth?

I call my sister even though I know that she has flown to Florida
for a bridge tournament. Modulated and proper, her taped voice
invites you to leave not only your name and number but also a time
when it would be convenient for her to return your call. "It's me
phoning you," I shout into the receiver. "I want points for this."
She is so nice, people have always said about her, their tone implying
that no one so otherwise perfect should have to be *nice* also. I am
the only one who knows the truth.

I cross my arms on Hugh's desk and rest my head on them. I
can't seem to clear it of Victor, Dana, the instructor, all talking at
once, trying to give me advice. At least Hugh was a quiet man. The
only thing he was ever stubborn about was not opening his mouth
unless he had something to say. My fingers go numb, my arms start
to ache, but I don't change position. I feel the hunch in my shoulders, the balls of my feet pushing against the floor—for how long?
I don't know. Time seems to stop. When I do move to rise, it's like
the first gasp of air after holding your breath.

As I bend to open the file drawer, something makes me pause
again—the muscular twist and extension at my waist—tells me to
hold the pose—feel the arc in my body, the drag of gravity on it—
let it fill a blank in my mind. Then for a longer time, because it is
an easy pose, I stand motionless, cradling a stack of files like a child
in my arms, my head tilted, face downcast. Then I am kneeling on

the hearth, stretching forever to place the stack on the grate. My spine is taut, my arms droop down like hemlock branches, waiting, waiting for the match to flash and swell into a quick hot flame.

I RUSH in late, after the instructor has begun to critique the homework assignment from the class I missed—self-portraits taped along the wall. He is teasing the older man, Forrest, about the proportions of his large-headed caricature—the broken pillar his figure leans its tiny elbow on is the same length as its nose. In the background is another ruined coliseum. Beside it Dana's drawing sort of quivers, dark and photographically real—a bed with a ruffled spread and a chest of drawers against a wallpaper background of ashen roses. Propped on the bed pillow sits a teddy bear with black button eyes and fur pencilled so thick it looks oily; on the chest is a small picture frame.

Abruptly stern, the instructor asks her, "Where are you in this?" She points to the empty frame, a diamond of white floating in heavy shade. She says she's not finished yet. "What about this bear?" he wants to know. Dana shrugs and tries to cover a pleading look with a smile. Below the outside corner of her left eye I notice an odd dent in the flesh, like a misplaced dimple. What the instructor sees is her leather vest, the combat boots. "No more teddy bears," he tells her, thinking she is strong enough to detect the compliment. "Not from you."

Her eyes flare. "You said we were supposed to draw for ourselves."

"Not you," he says. "Not yet."

There is no Victor this evening, instead a young woman with a cold. She keeps a Ziploc sandwich bag of remedies on the shelf behind her chair. She rests one knee on its seat and drapes one arm along its back. During our breaks, she wraps in a blanket, sprays her throat, sniffs an inhaler, and applies Vaseline to the chapped area under her nose. It annoys me that Forrest has taken the easel next to mine. He is working too slowly. For long minutes he stands there as still as the model, as if his heart has stopped. I want to tell him to stop ogling her breasts. Their fixed symbols stare out from his tablet like two bulging eyes. I want to snap in half that ultra-sharp pencil he wouldn't part with; I am tired of his figures all turning out like cartoons. He renders the stretch marks on the model's belly with two sets of wiggly lines.

"There are no lines in nature," the instructor tells him.

We are supposed to be paying attention to light, noting its absence. I like doing this. I am reasonably successful at blurring forms, scanning the shadows, brushing their pattern onto a rippling page with washes of watered ink.

On Forrest's other side, Dana is getting more and more upset with the smattering of blotches in front of her. She makes angry noises, rips the page from her tablet, balls it up and crushes it with her boot. The instructor ambles over and watches her start again. "There's no need to surrender the form completely," he says, flipping his fist into an open hand. "It's a matter of balancing what you know is there against what the light lets you see."

"I don't see anything," she grumbles.

"It's not important how one drawing turns out," the instructor reminds her. "What's important is the experience."

"I don't need this experience," Dana says, groping in her satchel for a cigarette.

He backs away and seems to address all of us though his voice gives up the minute she leaves the room. "Shadows are relatively minor truths, but they can be very distracting, even seductive. It takes time to learn to resist them and stay faithful to the truth of form."

"MAYBE you should listen to the instructor," I tell Dana after keeping my silence for most of the drive to her bungalow. The arms clenched across her chest, that gaze out the side window—it is a pose I could draw from memory—the inconsolable child.

"You mean, maybe I should quit."

"I think you know that's not what I mean. He's saying you don't have to try so hard." She glares at me as if I am crazy. "You must know he thinks you're good."

"Sure. That's why all that stuff he says just goes—"She skims an open palm over the top of her head. "I don't see why he won't just let us draw however we want and not have to think about so much stuff."

Her sullenness gets to me. "This is a college course, remember. Not summer camp."

I can see what she will do before she does it—bounce around in her seat, into that pose of attack. "What do you know about summer camp?"

"Here's your street," I say.

"I bet you sent your kids to summer camp. I bet they begged you not to make them go, and you paid no attention."

I pull the car to the curb. The house begins to bark. "I wasn't talking about summer camp," I say. "I was talking about your enormous potential." I have to clear my throat of that sad word. "You've got more than anyone else in the class." Had I really believed there might be some potential left in me, one last neglected seed waiting to sprout?

"My mother got off a bunch of prayers about me living up to my potential, the whole time she's signing me into rehab. Next thing I know there's this chick sitting on my chest, slapping the shit out of my face."

I refuse to be slapped into silence. "Today was an off day for you," I say. "But you've got plenty of other days ahead."

"Slapped the shit out of me because I was screaming and tearing up my bed," Dana says, before she gets out of the car and slams the door.

"YOU'RE ready to take the plunge," my sister concludes, because I who have never initiated lunch initiated this one. Already I regret it. She is just back from her bridge tournament in Orlando, where she won enough gold points to qualify for Life Master; she is acting bossier than ever. "We can go check if the place is still available as soon as we've eaten. But really, I can't imagine that it won't be. Sales always drop off in the middle of winter. No one wants to move now."

"Then why is it on the market now?"

"You don't always have a choice, you know. The reality is that most of the homes here turn over because their owners pass away."

Across the cavernous Pavilion the February sun streams in through the eight French doors along one wall, casting ghostly spots on the brittle bodies trapped at the tables there. I think my sister has a way of announcing reality without ever feeling it.

"Why am *I* supposed to want to move now, and how am I supposed to sell my house now?"

"If you would forget about arguing, we could make plans."

"That's not why I'm here," I say. My sister gives me an exasperated look. It deepens as I tell her the little I know about Dana and the run-down place she calls a *group home*.

"She's lucky to be there," my sister says. "And you of all people should stay out of it. Good lord, if I had a dollar for every young person I've lectured about substance abuse, I'd be a rich woman. You know as well as I do, there isn't anything you can say."

"She's all alone," I tell her. My sister nods, as though she, who never married, never failed as a mother or daughter, had cornered that reality also. "She has so much talent, and no one to encourage her. She's going to give up."

"I take it this art class is what you meant by going back to school?"

I produce the tube of drawings I have brought to show her and begin unrolling it. She takes one look at Victor naked, grabs the pages, rerolls them in jerks, saying, "Not here, for heaven's sake. What on earth are you thinking?"

"You should see what Dana does. It's amazing."

"Is this a *black* man?" She looks down at the cylinder of paper in her hands, amazed enough.

I say, "All our lives this has been going on, and we didn't know it."

"What makes you think—"

"Every day in these secret classrooms, human beings are taking off all their clothes and holding very still in strange positions, which is harder to do than you'd think, probably harder than strenuous exercise, and other human beings are drawing them in these positions, trying to save their bodies on paper—all the curves and folds, lumps, bulges, scars, hair, even their toe nails."

My sister lays down her fork. "I can't eat if you're going to go on in that crazy way."

"I simply wanted you to know," I say. "It's a whole other world."

My sister is sitting back as much as I am leaning forward. "How I wish," she says with stiff jaws, "that you would start living in the real one."

"I have been thinking about offering Dana a room in my house."

"That idea is worse than ridiculous, it's immoral," my sister says, standing up and shouldering her purse. "It won't solve her problems and it will compound your own."

I ARRIVE for the next class a few minutes late and Dana is not there. The instructor is brusquely passing out black paper and white crayons. He snaps at a girl for beginning to doodle before he has told us what we are to do. He stops at my easel and deliberately watches me remove my poncho and muffler. When I have settled myself on a stool, he asks to see the self-portrait I missed. I tell him I haven't had a chance to get to it. I don't mention that I have tried to draw myself drawing myself in front of three different mirrors but never finished, couldn't finish. Each time I saw the same stiff, flat contours take shape on my tablet, the prim head, round shoulders and crossed knees, I was overcome with disgust.

The instructor warns me that the self-portrait is a required assignment. He keeps glancing at the outside door, as if he resents me for being here when Dana isn't, as if somehow her absence were my fault.

Victor emerges from the inside door wrapped in his old sheepskin and I am surprised at the slight surge along my nerves as he shuffles barefoot toward the front of the room. He seems to sense the instructor's distraction. He makes a point of checking out the black sheet of paper in front of each of us. "This some kind of racial slur?" he asks with a glassy grin. He sheds his coat and takes his first pose on the platform, one foot planted behind the other, right arm raised as if he's about to throw something. The instructor sets up a spotlight at an angle behind him. "That's fine," Victor says. "Watusi hunter at sunset." The instructor nods and finally smiles.

We are to draw the light on Victor's skin, to conjure his form onto the black paper by means of light. I move calmly enough from the face, almost backlit, indistinct, to the neck, where a lozenge of light catches one ridge of collarbone. I begin to feel the tension in the lifted shoulder. And then I remember what lies ahead: the sunken chest, the withered, dangling scrotum, that knee, the entire defenseless body, in all its transient, dense detail. I know it is all waiting there below the neck no matter what pattern the light tricks me into seeing. Then I hear the instructor say, "Give it up, Forrest, for Christsake. Outlines aren't the answer."

The strength goes out of my arm and I can't continue. I have no gift to bring to this work, and the one with the gift isn't here.

It seems to give everyone else a boost of energy and purpose when the instructor cuts the class short. In the midst of the bustling and loud banter, I am so tired that I sink into a chair and prop my head in my hand. When I close my eyes I see myself getting into my car, driving. Up ahead is the turn, the hill down to that house, but I cannot see myself getting there, making my way through the clutter on the porch, braving the angry dog. And hovering somewhere in the picture is Dana's face, bitter and righteous, ready to say no to anything I suggest. Before we parted outside the Pavilion, my sister announced that I wasn't going to get my own children back by meddling in the affairs of strangers. "You did the best you could," she told me. "No," I said, because she is always so comfortable and wrong, "I just did."

The instructor stands over me, clearing his throat. He's got his parka on, a cigarette tucked behind one ear. We gaze at each other skeptically.

"She may not be as tough as you think she is," I say finally.

For a minute he pretends he doesn't know what I'm talking about. Then he says stiffly, "If she's the real thing, she'll be back."

"And if she isn't?" He shrugs off my question. "Is that reason to give up on her?"

"Where are you in this?" His question, abrupt and stern, reminds me of Dana's picture of an empty picture and for a minute I think I might be going to cry.

"I don't know," I say. "I'm sitting right here. Maybe I'm waiting for Victor."

His frown tells me there is some sort of policy this goes against. "Is that wise?" he asks me, who could be his mother.

"No," I answer, all at once sure. "It is worse than ridiculous, it is immoral." Just then Victor appears. The instructor tries to throw him a warning look, but Victor's sleepy eyes just let it drop. "I was wondering," I say to Victor—it takes all my will to sound cheerful and sociable—"did you ever get that business straightened out with your Social Security?"

"I guess I did," Victor says emphatically. The instructor makes a loud noise of frustration and is gone. I begin collecting my belongings. "But you know they've still got me waiting on those back checks. Living pretty close to the bone."

I toss my poncho over my head but it catches on my glasses and I lose the neck hole. I am groping in the dark when I feel Victor tug the heavy cloth down and into place. "Let me buy you coffee or dinner or something," I say.

"I don't guess that will be necessary," he says.

"I didn't mean that the way maybe you think I might have," I say. "You'd be doing me the favor." He looks at me expressionless. "You could at least let me drive you home." He shakes his head at the floor.

VICTOR lives in the city in an old apartment building that has seen more elegant days. In between spitting bits of directions at me, he stares out his side window, ill at ease. I can't seem to draw him out. Then I pull up in front of the entrance, and he turns on me and demands, "How come you're not afraid of me? You scare the hell out of me. You're white, you're female, and"—he softens his voice tactfully—"maybe you're a little off."

I say, "Can we forget black white and man woman and present future, is that possible?"

"Where you been living all your life?"

"Victor, I'm sixty years old and I've done everything wrong," I say.

He tucks his long chin into his neck then looks at me sidelong. "I guess there's no cause for changing now."

WE share a carton of sweet-and-sour pork at an old dinette table of formica and chrome. Victor takes a long time chewing each bite, and deflects my questions with flat humor. He has been married, but who hasn't? He has no children anyone could pin on him. He's traveled, enough to know that one cheap motel with lumpy bed is the same as another.

At the other end of the room, away from the single ceiling light, a sagging Danish Modern sofa and a slatted coffee table sit opposite two speakers the size of footlockers. There is a record player on the table. The walls are covered with pictures in every medium, in assorted styles, of varying skill. Despite the shadows, I think I recognize Victor in all of them.

"What's it like," I try again, "to be an artist's model?"

"You really into this Barbara Walters thing?" Victor asks back.

"I was wondering if maybe it felt a little strange living with all these pictures. Everywhere you look you see yourself."

Victor works at detaching and unbending the wire handle on our food carton. "Maybe I don't look at them as *myself*. If other folks make them, and then give them to me, I guess I look at them as gifts. Who knows?" He starts probing his long teeth with the straightened wire. "The world being what it is, maybe one or two'll be worth a few bucks one of these days."

After another silence I say, "What I'm into is keeping you talking so I won't have to go home." Victor's heavy mouth tenses with pained politeness. "Don't worry," I assure him. "You won't be stuck with me. My life is a little up in the air at the moment, but I'm fine." He resumes poking his teeth. "Do you think you can tell if a picture is good?"

He stops and studies me for a minute. "I don't try," he says.

"I wasn't going to ask about *my* pictures. I know mine are pretty blah. I mean, I've always enjoyed drawing, but it's not as if it was even a hobby particularly. I signed up for the class because I thought my life needed the structure and so my sister wouldn't think I was letting myself go." I am meaning to talk to him about Dana, *her* pictures, her potential; it's as if she floats just ahead of my voice and I can't quite break away and catch up with her. "But that's not really true. The truth is that I signed up because my mother once called me artistic. She called me lots of things—selfish, stubborn, undependable, amoral—but once I overheard her tell a friend of hers I was artistic. Can you believe that? So here I am almost half a century later. Isn't it amazing what a little encouragement can do?"

I do not raise a chuckle from Victor. "You know it doesn't matter if you're not good?" he asks.

"What matters is whether you're young," I say.

He shrugs. "You do what you got to do when you got to do it," he says.

"It's much harder than I thought it would be," I say, remembering the self-portrait I may never manage. Victor nods and as I follow his gaze around his walls, it dawns on me. "You're in this too, aren't you?" He cocks his long head, perplexed. "Drawing pictures."

"Guess you could call it that," he says.

"I've got a feeling you're good. Tell me, which of these are self-portraits?"

He shrugs again. "I don't work with all that paper and paint. I work with air." He smiles, for now I am puzzled. He lifts those graceful fingers in the direction of a large unframed canvas over the sofa, a portrait of himself in shades of blue. Balanced in indigo hands a brighter blue column curves up to his puffed out indigo cheeks. "I play sax," he says. I still don't get it. "I make music. You know—with all that natural rhythm? Jazz?"

"Where?" is all I can think to ask.

"Wherever. These days, mostly right here." He gets up and

crosses to a seat on the couch, and drags first a black case then a grocery carton full of records out from under it. He opens the case and takes up the horn; it gleams across his knees like a source of light. He walks his fingers through the albums, extracts one, and places it on the turntable. "I jam with the best," he says.

"Don't," I say, startling him. "I mean the record. I'd rather hear just you by yourself."

His smile stiffens the way it did when I said I didn't want to go home. Then his expression lifts. "How about I draw you?" He slips the mouthpiece between his lips and blows a chilly ripple of notes, like a downhill skid into gloom. "Come on," he coaxes, taking a spot between the speakers away from the light. "You go stand over there," he cocks his head toward an opposite corner.

"I think maybe now I am afraid," I say.

He plays the same run of notes. "You mean *that?*" He shakes his head. "I guess that one's been around for a long time." I don't move. "That's fine," he says, "you hold real still and I draw you right there." I heave myself to my feet. "Hey, I said *still*," Victor calls. "You think drawing's hard work, time you tried the other side of the picture."

"I'm embarrassed. I should go." I feel caught under the light.

"That's fine," he says. "Be embarrassed."

I cross my arms across my chest and hunch over, head bowed. The horn makes short bleats and then that ripple of notes again dropping into the dark. More bleats slap at my ears, then give way to mixed-up honking, like stalled traffic. The noise gets louder, more chaotic. I cover my ears with my hands, close my eyes, try to imagine distractions, but I can still hear the sound, which organizes itself now into something low and throaty and arrogant. *I see you,* it says, *no matter how much you wish you could hide, I see you. I see everything you have done and not done.* I clench every muscle to block it out, but the tighter I clench, the more determined Victor plays.

All at once, I cannot fight anymore, my muscles are screaming for me to give up. The instant my arms drop to my sides, the sound breaks off. I raise my head and there is melody, unfamiliar but flowing smooth and lovely, and Victor nodding as he plays.

Damp with sweat, I slip off my cardigan and clutch it to my chest like a shield, and the melody rises flutelike, and I am willing to stand like that forever, with its sweetness fluttering toward me, but Victor, my new instructor, stops long enough to call, "Change." For a moment, the fear comes back—how to choose a new pose, the right pose, from among all possible poses, freely choose? What I do is keep moving, take off my glasses and place them on the table, slowly bend and untie my sensible shoes. I am getting ready. I bunch off each wool sock, for I crave the grip of the cold floor on my feet.

The music doesn't falter, but slows and shifts into a minor key. I peer over at Victor up against his dark wall, I think his eyes are shut. He is swaying back and forth, drawing pictures with his breath. I'm not sure they are pictures of me anymore, these notes bruised with sadness, yet they call to me, promising relief. I undo my slacks and let them slide to the floor, I pull off my turtleneck. Shyly, I look down at my own body, and I want to cry and laugh—it has surrendered form so completely, yet form seems such vanity, such a minor truth. I go ahead and unhook the brassiere with the shot elastic, and as I let down my empty breasts, I think how blind children are, how spellbound by grievance and blame. When I am naked I stretch my hands out in front of me palms up, not to reach for Victor, or anyone in particular, but simply to see how long I will be able to hold them still and unsupported in midair.

Holiday

S O many of us are ugly. As if we were chosen for that. Ugly giants with bulging bellies and rumps, pallid skin inflamed by the sun. Then there are the others who rock their slow way across the sand in socks and canvas shoes, balancing beer bottles on trays, Styrofoam cups of rum punch. Or serve us grilled shrimp in garlic sauce under a thatched roof. Or give us our daily beach towels. Or make our beds and fold the torn ends of our toilet paper into points. Or mop the marble floors. These others are so small and tawny you want to touch them. But their uniforms are a pristine white, like hospital orderlies, and many clasp walkie-talkies.

Still waking to clocks at home, we are on the beach early. Paul leaves on his terry robe and settles his bulk into one upright chair in the shade of a leafy umbrella; I perch on another. I have brought #15 sunscreen. He has brought Henry James. As he finds his place, I stroke on the goo. Slowly he remembers to stretch his heavy lips into a smile. "This isn't Paris, is it," he says in that mournful tone of his. "Or even San Remo." He is doing this for me. I have lost a breast, and he is trying to give me anything I want.

"Let's just say it's different," I suggest, protecting him as usual. What this certainly isn't is a conference, or a place with museums, a library housing special collections. "There's no point in making comparisons," I say as plump, discrete clouds sail by overhead like a procession of powdered wigs.

In the middle of the beach, a pantomime stutters in the yielding sand. A man in white is showing a boy in white how to line up the scattered chaises two by two. The boy goes to work with all the gestures of efficiency, but when he has almost finished the job, he realizes there will be an odd chaise left over. Perplexed, he looks up and down the beach but there is no sign of his boss. So he just collapses, legs splayed, onto the sand and sifts it first through his right fingers, then his left.

The Golden Bowl has closed on Paul's thumb, come to rest on his thigh. With the other hand he combs back the forelock of straight gray hair that always falls over his eyes. He is watching the boy too. Then the book jerks erect and Paul looks across at me. As his eyebrow lifts, so do my nerves. This is what we do well—be amused together.

The next minute, I can't see anything, I have stood up too fast, but I stumble anyway toward the boy, toward the lone chaise, grab its back, ask, "May I take this leftover one?" He doesn't seem to understand. I explain to him with my other hand how I—my entire body—would like to stretch itself along the plastic webbing after I drag it over there nearer that large, pale man.

The boy is on his feet in a flash, nodding, thanking me, then in a frenzy of sand he churns back toward the hotel.

"I suppose the prospect of some sort of tip necessarily colors everything they do," Paul suggests to the pages of his book.

I lie on my stomach in the sun and close my eyes. Did I really see that boy's smile, so sudden, unconditional, free?

YES, I am ugly, it's the right word for a fact I have come to accept. When I was young I swore by Estee Lauder. I learned how to paint bigger eyes, fuller lips, how to highlight cheekbones that hardly exist and hide a bump on my nose you can't miss. But the whole time I heard laughter, like background noise—*look at that stupid girl, isn't she pathetic, she thinks she can work a miracle, not a chance.* And now it's the same with this custom-made breast they showed me how to stick in my bra. Maybe I should have said no right off. Thanks but no thanks. It's not as if I've lost a leg, or my kidneys, something you've got to replace. It's more like a brooch or necklace, a bauble—the right word again. Of what use are baubles to an ugly woman like me?

PAUL was fifty, a full professor when we met. When he plopped down an armload of books on the library counter in front of me, then proceeded to dribble the contents of his trouser pockets and wallet onto the floor. When I came out from behind the desk and stooped to join him, to help pick things up. Where our eyes met for a moment, his brimming with panic and apology. When and where I noticed the corner of his library card peeking from the breast pocket of his jacket like a crisp handkerchief, and reached over and plucked it out.

Then the large, slack jaw and mouth, the eyes sunk into flesh the color of bruise, that whole distracted face pulled together in gratitude, and suddenly the man who bumbled around campus like a joke, getting locked in his office overnight or lost on his way to class, this man I had chuckled at along with the other librarians had stirred up my heart, unburied scraps of hope.

I knew I was too old to think about children. I just needed to be reminded. The first time he broached marriage, he said, "I have no desire to leave my name on anything but a body of ideas."

What we forgot sipping Chardonnay and turning up the volume on *Carmina Burana* came back to mock us: it was a little late for nakedness, it seemed unnatural, we didn't know what to do. The desire to be carried away is not desire.

"It's similar," Paul said, "to having a particularly significant thought yet being unable to express it for lack of the right words." He was sitting up on the edge of the bed in the dark. I lay behind him, staring at the shadow of his broad, soft back, too mortified to speak. "I'm sorry if I have let you down," he said. "Our companionship is more important to me than any carnal acrobatics." His declaration sounded like a question. I couldn't answer. I wasn't sure whether an important companionship was better than nothing at all.

IT isn't the breast *per se,* it's the space between the two of them, the mysterious crease, the sign of risen flesh, yeasty and warm. What is the sound of one hand clapping? Where is the allure of a single breast?

The people who engineer bathing suits know all about this—how to create the deepest crease. The wildest promise. The suit I am wearing says, *Don't even bother to think about it.* It has a high neck, broad straps, bones to keep my plastic bag of gel in line. Still I am afraid to swim in the sea, afraid that the currents, my flailing arms will spring the thing loose, it will float off like a fish gone pale belly up. Instead I trudge up to the pool deck, Paul usually following. We wade in, bend our knees until the lukewarm water reaches our necks, inhale the odor of chlorine, and wade out again.

WHEN they told me there would have to be surgery, I said *Take them both, take everything, I'm not interested in options, I don't care.* I wasn't thinking of increasing my chances for survival. I was making noise—my wounds would speak where I couldn't, cry out, shock Paul into noticing me. Or maybe I thought removing my breasts would punish him for never caring whether they yearned for him or not.

In the hospital he picked up my hand, the one I was having to strain to lift by myself, and pressed it to his lips. "This doesn't change anything," he said, meaning to be kind. Closing the file on my loss. Putting it away next to his malformed vertebrae, his diverticulitis, and his allergies to pollen and leaf mould, in the drawer marked *Silence.* "Don't ask," he told me one morning years ago, the last time I wondered aloud how he was feeling. "You may simply assume that I am always in pain."

| | |

EACH morning the same omelette, laden with peppers, tomatoes, and spicy meat. The coffee reminds me of canned spinach. In the squat tree beyond the dining terrace: leaves like shiny green saucers, lizards the size of spoons.

After breakfast, Paul's belly rumbles, and he is a different man, almost vivacious, giddy. The slap-slap of his rubber sandals quickens. Will he make it back to the room? This is proof of our intimacy, his trust, that as we race-walk the marble corridor side by side, he farts freely.

Later on the beach, the same arrangement, him sitting under the umbrella, slack and pale, reading; me prone in the sun. Paul pages slowly through the last centimeter of his book. I know, because he has told me, that he savors every word, entranced by the complexity of every sentence, the shifting levels. Women flounce past—some with all the right creases on display, some with all the wrong ones—at least he never looks up. I turn my face toward the familiar water. For days I've been lying here trying to think of its other names. I have thought of ink for the distance, frothed milk for the pools among the rocks, and for the middle range that cool, almost crisp jelly you find inside certain chocolates. But none of these has brought satisfaction, relief.

Time is running out.

After the mammogram, when they said the doctor would like to speak to me in her office, my mind guessed those words.

The pressure of that synthetic lump against my scars is uncomfortable. If I turn over on my back it sticks up like a fist. Time is running out and where am I? In the wrong body, with the wrong man, the wrong words? The crescent where my breast was is a mouth that cries *no*.

Later when we are back in our room, Paul will request an explanation for what I do next. Will he pity my simplicity, my ignorance of subtlety, shifting levels when all I can say is *People do what they do when they are ready?*

I roll onto my left side, work my right hand down the top of my bathing suit, and peel the mound from my chest. I sit up, pulling it into view, translucent, malleable—the way it fills up your hand, you can't help squeezing it. I feel dizzy, off balance. As if something is on the verge of turning inside out. So I reach for Paul, grab what's closest, his big toe, and hang on to that until he looks up. He frowns and sort of shakes his foot, but I smile and can't let go. When he notices what's in my other hand, I dandle it in the air between us, and the clear little knob of a nipple makes me laugh. Then he gives a hard kick—I never thought he had it in him—his horny toenail digs right into my palm, and he gasps, "My God, what's gotten into you?" Then he sets his book aside, lumbers over and puts his hands on my shoulders. "I'm sorry," he says. "I have tried to imagine how you must feel—"

"Do you have to imagine? Can't you just see?" I am looking right into the cavity of his navel. I wave the breast over my head.

"I see it, I see. That doesn't mean I can understand."

I HAVE stuck the expensive breast in a sanitary napkin bag, then into the trash. I tell Paul that I am tired of the hotel's mandatory fiesta every night, all those whining guitars, I am going to take a cab into the town to look for something closer to real life. I'd like to tell him he doesn't have to come, but I know he must, to prove that he would do anything for me.

We have dinner outdoors where we can watch families stroll the twilit plaza, the smallest children dressed up like brides and grooms. I devour the shrimp in garlic sauce I've come to crave. Paul has ordered a platter of rice heaped with mollusks and various tentacles edged with suckers, rings of octopus, and whole squid no bigger than a medium thumb. He can't resist shaking one of these in my face, and I can't help flinching. Then he slowly sucks the thing headfirst into his mouth. Though the lines in his brow are set for complaint, a giggle escapes him. He pokes around for another squid, his eyes twinkling up at me through straight, gray lashes.

"Wasn't this a good idea? Aren't we having a good time?" I ask, which is all it takes to bring him down.

While we eat, the bandstand in the middle of the square is being taken over by a squad of men in red-and-yellow striped ponchos. They carry up speakers the size of coffins, guitars and trumpets in cases, an assortment of naked drums. As they set up their equipment, more men in plain clothes wedge themselves onto the platform, sit on the railing, hang over it, or scramble from it onto the flattened cone of a roof. You'd think they'd heard word of a flood.

At 8:17 by Paul's watch the bells of the church in one corner chime eight, one of the men in ponchos raises a trumpet to his lips and blares a long, jagged warning, and the inevitable music begins to whine. I pretend not to notice Paul's tolerant, self-righteous smirk.

Half a dozen older girls in tube miniskirts and high heels pair off and sway at the base of the bandstand. Littler children escape parents and burst onto the open concrete, skip and twirl, shove and chase, a ballet of tiny suits and patent shoes and frilly monolithic dresses with lives of their own. Soon the large-boned, sunburned men and women from the North come prancing out of the shadows like acts of God, two by two, in Bermuda shorts and T-shirts. Some jitterbug, some shake like palsy. The smug, passionless ones have been to Arthur Murray and know exactly what to do.

We have finished the wine and Paul is figuring the tip when I realize the man standing next to our table is there for a reason. He is the color and fragrance of dark honey, he wears a starched white shirt, its top buttons open, and sharply creased, flared pants. He could be any age, but he must be the tallest inhabitant of this town.

Now Paul is also aware of the man, and the man realizes this, and makes a small bow. He looks from me to Paul and back. I wrap my linen blazer more tightly across my chest. Paul keeps combing his hand through the hair on his brow, forgets to close his lips, and the lower one droops moistly.

With a warm smile, the man wonders, "Would the senora care to dance?"

I try to smile back, stammering, "Gracias. No thank you."

"This is very fine music," the man says, like a question. His neck is very short. To look over at the bandstand he must turn his whole body. Then he turns back to Paul and me. The way he is sort of shuffling in place makes his hips sort of twitch. My ears feel hot.

"I am not a dancer," I explain politely.

"I can teach you," he says. "All can learn."

"No. Please," I say, as if the stranger were twisting my arm, when it is Paul who has clambered to his feet, clutching my elbow, who is steering me off toward the main avenue along the water.

"It wouldn't surprise me if he were being paid to do that," Paul says, when we reach the curb. "By the Tourist Bureau or something."

"To do what?"

Paul bites his lip. "You must have noticed how handsome he was," he says after a pause. He lifts his hand and a red cab squirts from a side alley and stops in front of us. He opens the door for me.

"I'm not ready to go," I say, looking down at my feet.

He pauses again before telling me, "Don't be insane."

"I would just like to look around a little longer."

"I don't suppose I can tell you that you won't find anything."

I am not myself. "How would you know? You never unstick your eyes from that book."

His face lengthens, his shoulders stoop even more. "Please, take your time," he says, as if his lower jaw were made of lead. "Take all the time in the world."

"I'm sorry," I say, in general.

He folds his bulk into the back of the compact cab. "When you reach my age," he says, "you realize that places are not as different as they may appear."

Without thinking I say, "Maybe I never will."

I AM not going to run back to the plaza, I am going to stroll along the waterfront. Cabs whizz past, the moon glows like a grimy headlight. On the pier entwined couples wait for a special boat to take them to their white ship anchored halfway to the horizon and strung with thousands of white lights, so bright you can read the name *HOLIDAY* scrolled large along the bow.

All at once I veer off down a side street. I don't know where I'm going, just know I must go fast. Block by block the shops and res-taurants begin shrinking, dimming, then run out. The air is thick with carbon monoxide, sulphur. Beat-up parked cars clog the side-walk, bicycles without lights pass in the dark, their tires sizzling softly. In the yards, sniffing the trash piles or dozing in the dirt, the same skinny no-color dog. Through open doorways and slat-ted windows I glimpse cupboards, tables, hammocks, bodies, hear the chatter and drone of TV. If someone happens to look out as I pass, I smile, say *Buenos noces*. I want to add, *I love you, I don't want to be afraid anymore.*

I start turning corners on instinct, finally stumble out onto a brightly lit street of shops and dressed-up people again, the faint echo of music—back to civilization, I think, meaning handwoven acrylic blankets, silver jewelry, Day-Glo T-shirts. The plaza opens up ahead, the bandstand moored like another dreamy ship on the sea of the crowd.

I swim my way through it, looking for the tall man, and then I see him dancing with someone else. She is a little heavy like me, not quite attractive, and just as clumsy as I would have been, but much more drunk. I feel faint, ashamed, as if I were out there my-self, wiggling my hips and stepping on my own feet. He is graceful, seductive but so contained he doesn't seem to notice her sidelong looks, or feel her cheek brush his neck. Or realize when the music stops that she would do anything not to be escorted back to the table where a fat man with a bald, pink head is devouring tortilla chips piled with guacamole.

I button up my blazer, smooth the lapels. As he moves away from their table, I step in front of him, too frightened to smile.

"Excuse, please," he says, gliding past.

"You are an excellent dancer," I say to his back.

He turns his whole body and gives me a stiff bow. "*Gracias, señora.*"

"You don't remember me," I say.

"I remember you," he says gallantly after the briefest pause.

"Well. Would you like me to, I don't know, maybe buy you a drink?"

"Oh no," he says with a pleasant laugh, as if the idea were a clever joke, as if he were not trying to get away.

"I realize you can't stop and socialize with every strange woman who tries to strike up a conversation, but just do me a favor, just answer one question for me, is that fair?"

He looks puzzled, tries another pleasant laugh. I realize with a flush of dismay how young he is.

"Does someone pay you to ask women to dance?"

He shrugs and holds out his arms to me, begins shuffling his feet.

"No, no," I say. "That's not what I meant. Besides, you are too handsome for that. And I am too old."

"My wife is very beautiful," he says.

I am surprised to feel relieved, as if someone had straightened a tilting picture or shut the door on a draught. "My husband thinks you do this for money."

His face brightens with comprehension. "Not for money," he says. "My English is very bad. I like to practice my English."

"Then you should talk to me instead of dancing. Tell me who you are, what you do."

His name is Jesus, and there is no *instead*. His feet move, his hips shift minutely with the rhythm of his speech—he is employed as assistant head waiter at the Fiesta Caribe, a four-star hotel, where he makes very good money, and if I bring my husband there to the restaurant tomorrow night, he will fix for us a most wonderful bananas flambé. Then he asks, "Do you live in Indiana?"

"No," I say, taken aback, "I'm from Philadelphia—"

"Do you have family in Indiana?" he interrupts.

He is fiercely serious—I wish I could help him. I think hard before I shake my head.

His dance has ceased. "My father lives in Indiana."

"Your father?"

It encourages him that I am amazed. "It's a very beautiful and wild place, Indian-a?"

All I can think of to say is, "Some may think so."

"When I find him he will have big surprise."

"Do you know his name?"

"Only Joe. What we say here *José*."

"There are so many Joes in Indiana," I say.

Jesus nods. "Some day it may be he comes back here. So I am waiting. I practice my English. It may be he brings his wife to the plaza to hear the excellent music. When I find her, she will have big surprise."

IT is our last day, hot as usual, but a wind has roiled the sea into surf. Waves whip the rocks along the shore with a one-two beat, whoosh, crack. Their spray stings my back like a sun shower as it's blown across the sand.

I have sewn flat one side of my bathing suit. Paul seems not to have noticed, maybe he just doesn't dare. He is lying low, being very kind, always a gentleman. Hoping that whatever got into me will work itself out. Last night I had a dream out of Jules Verne: me alone in a diving bell, leagues under the sea, watching a crack in the steel wall widen, a trickle of water become a pour.

I push myself up. After those weeks of exercises, my right arm is as strong as it will ever be. "I'm going for a swim," I say.

Paul raises his face, a look both solicitous and blank.

"I'd like some money," I say. "To rent one of those masks and those rubber things you put on your feet."

"I'm sorry," Paul says. "I was completely absorbed—"

I repeat myself.

"It is so difficult to move from this world"—he taps his book—"into this." He looks around him as if for the first time. "It's so garish." He rubs one large veined foot against the other. "And sandy."

"I think they cost ten," I say.

"You understand, it has nothing to do with you," he says. "Why if it weren't for you, I might never—"

"I understand," I say. Last night he confessed to me what *he* would never understand—how I could have any affection for him whatsoever.

He gazes at the inky horizon. "I could be persuaded to take a dip in the pool," he says.

"Afterward," I say.
"Of course," he says.

I AM whapping along the concrete jetty in my flippers and mask, mouth-breathing through the attached tube. If people are staring at me, I can't see them. If there are others in swimming, I don't see them either.

I lower myself down the ladder, and the current grabs me, lifts and drops me along its choppy surface, threatens to fling me back against the pier. I kick and claw the waves, and the flippers are a surprise, they have made my legs strong, equal to the strength of the sea. I hardly need my arms. I put my mask into the water, which is cloudy with sand. Poor blue striped fish the size of my hand are being knocked backward by the currents, jerked up and down, their round eyes dazed. But I can make out the pale sandy bottom only a meter or two underneath me, and it is moving: I am kicking steadily forward.

Farther from shore the water clears. Strange shapes jut from the sandy bottom—purple lacey fans swaying back and forth, golden hands waving their dozens of furry fingers, knobs of rusty brains. What look like giant hunks of porous lava teem with fish, a dazzle of shapes and color, silver, black, striped and speckled, trimmed with reds and golds and luminous blues.

There is one fish so beautiful I stop breathing, trying to hold still—a vibrant green with fins and tail like rainbows, the size of a small child. It keeps butting against the porous rock, its mouth gropes, digs. I can't believe I've been allowed a glimpse of something so gorgeous. I paddle to keep up with it, but after a while it veers away from its feeding, as though to shake me off, a shadow in its sky.

Such excitement uses energy—but really it doesn't take much to stay afloat in these waters. I spend a little more on panic when I can't locate the shore. The waves keep rising like dares to block my line of sight, and my mask, transparent against water, fogs in the air.

But my feet tread as though they could forever, and when the crest of a wave gives me a lift, I can make out something floating not far off, an orange globe, some sort of buoy. I tip my face back into the water: a thick encrusted cable angles down from the buoy, and around its upper part have gathered hundreds of yellow fish, all heading the same direction. Each keeps the same two or three inches distance from every other. None moves but all move as the current lifts and lowers the mass of them, swings them around an unseen pole.

Cold fish. The words surprise, make me laugh, gulp a full sobering taste of salt. I shiver. An urge sends me swimming right into the school, grabbing to right and left, cursing until my head could burst with its own noise.

It isn't particularly fast that they part and glide out my way, but fast enough, as if they can read not my mind—something else. I want to be in their midst, feel just one of them bump into me, squeeze its springy flesh against my palm. But my hands keep closing on thin water. As if what has brought us together holds us apart.

Then the burst of energy is spent. I am calm. There is no such thing as effort. I see my body shrink to a sliver. My legs, lithe in their flippers, stroke the water like proper fins. The buoy is a tiny planet with rings of yellow moons. It bobs above a ledge, where the sandy floor drops off. Beyond it, the water's as deep as all the time in the world, and as dark.

The Only Way
to Ride

THEY had married in May, in the midst of a premature hot spell that withered the azaleas almost the minute the shrubs bloomed, the kind of weather, Nan thinks now, that makes people do crazy things—lean on car horns and shout obscenities and panic at the emptiness of their lives.

She'd hardly known him. There had been three dinners, then a comfortable weekend together, after which Will had flashed that ready smile of his—appreciative, condescending, heedless—and proposed. "If you're going to do something," he'd said, "you ought to do it right."

"I don't know about right," Nan said. Will was too handsome, too outgoing, too old; he had been married too often. They had nothing in common but the endodontist in whose waiting room they had met—she was facing a root canal for the first time, he had just survived one. Besides, Will had a problem he was desperate to fix—a daughter, Angela. Had Nan been flattered by his hope that she could help him? What had she meant when she conceded, "But maybe it's time"?

She and Will drove straight from the courthouse out to one of the further suburbs, to the tract of pastel townhomes that had sprung up on the ruins of an old farm, where Angela lived with her mother, Terri.

Will and Nan were made to stand too long on the narrow stoop, he in his brand-new suit, she in an unbleached muslin dress, the sun like a huge scorching spotlight exposing the vanity of it all. With her eyes, Nan tried to tell Will that she wanted to leave. Will gave an absurd, mechanical laugh. "Don't hold this against me," he said. "I never could walk away from a mistake."

The woman who finally answered the door was only a little older than Nan. She wore velour shorts, a tank top and a deep suntan, except for her face, which, framed by waves of dark hair, looked tired and faded, like a *before* picture in one of those articles about cosmetic makeovers. There was a little tuft of cotton between each of her toes and the nails on one foot were a glossy red. "Fancy meeting you here," Terri said to Will, sweeping Nan out of the picture with a disdainful glance. "Did you think she'd be sitting in the foyer waiting? I'm beside myself. I don't care if I never see her again. You—"

But Will had Nan by the arm and was guiding her back to the car. He was breathing loudly; a flush had darkened his features, muddled their confidence. And through the blur in her mind, Nan wondered what she'd gotten herself into.

After almost an hour of random, sometimes reckless cruising from one new shopping strip to another, they found her in a 7-Eleven parking lot, Angela attended by half a dozen friends, all sheathed in black despite the heat, leaning against an old Mustang with a cloudy finish, smoking cigarettes. Nan faced classrooms full of these malcontents every day, even managed to teach them a few things about thesis statements, personification, tragic flaws. Then what was there to be so nervous about now?

Pale makeup, blue-black eyeliner, and grape lipstick couldn't hide Angela's perfect features or her shock when she recognized the tall, gray-haired man in the suit as her father. Will approached slowly, murmuring greetings. Nan tiptoed behind him in her Guatemalan folk dress, drenched now with sweat, clutching the last-minute bridal bouquet of narcissus and forget-me-nots. The funereal lineup froze and went silent. Nan could feel their fear.

"I've got something to show you," Will said, his voice unexpectedly calm, firm.

Angela threw Nan the same dismissive look her mother had.

Will chuckled indulgently. "This is Nan. We've both got a surprise for you, if you want to hop in the car."

Angela's friends were watching her. The spiked mane of her hair fell in front of her face as she looked down at her pointed boots, shuffled them on the hot, oil-stained asphalt, shifting her weight. Nan found herself wanting to cry out, *Believe him, trust him, help him, help us all.* Instead she took a step forward, extending the flowers. Angela peeked up through her hair, then, almost as though she couldn't stop herself, her arms reached for the bouquet while her eyes quizzed her father's. "Something else," he said again, shaking his head. And then it happened. A stiffness in the girl broke, went slack. She let her father put his arm across her shoulders, she went with them. Will winked at Nan over his daughter's head.

WHAT Will had done was buy Angela the palomino Brandy and arrange to board it on a surviving farm only minutes from her house. As a child Angela had gone through a horse stage, read horse books, collected horse figurines; she had taken riding lessons too, until her parents, in the confusion of splitting up, began forgetting to drive her there. The plan now was to interest Angela in riding again, provide an outlet for her energy.

In the car, Will asked Angela questions about school which she answered automatically, with no particular regard for the truth. When they pulled into the farm, Angela had to be coaxed from the car, teased out of her lethargy long enough to cross the lawn to the barn, but as they started down the row of stalls, glimpsing in their dim shadows the contours of horses, her face began to twitch. She finally gave in to a smile that seemed to Nan almost smug. Soon the girl was giggling like a child and offering up the tender heads of Nan's daffodils to Brandy's mobile lips.

After that Will was in heaven, setting up riding lessons, replacing his daughter's black stretch jeans and torn shirts with suede-trimmed britches, a snappy green jacket. Sundays Angela abandoned her friends, removed the jumble of earrings from each lobe, wound her chaotic hair into a prim french braid and sat up stunningly straight in the saddle. After only a month they were towing the horse in a rented trailer to one local show or another. By the time school started in the fall, they'd won their first ribbon. If Nan never saw any real point to all that scrubbing and grooming and trotting around in the sawdust, she was still amazed. Riding, Angela seemed transformed. Her sullenness settled into concentration; her apathy became in the saddle a lovely centered nonchalance.

That year of weekends seems almost like a dream to Nan now — the three of them like the family she'd never had as a child, and never let the grown-up woman hope for. Will and Angela fussed over Brandy, then Will and Nan waited and watched, sipping from a thermos of steaming coffee or a jug of lemonade once the weather warmed again. Wherever they parked the horse trailer, they pitched their brief camp, and Nan unpacked sandwiches, muffins, fruit, and it never bothered her that everything tasted faintly of leather and dung. Thinking back, Nan wonders if she'd really expected such times could last.

Angela became almost vivacious, if too polite. She complimented Nan on outfits picked straight out of L. L. Bean, asked her about her students. Nan got the feeling that Angela used their conversations to practice various facial expressions — respect, solicitude, disbelief.

"You know, you don't have to take care of me," Nan mustered the courage to say one Sunday, when Will had gone off to check the scores and they had lapsed into silence. "It's all right with me if you aren't always *on*. You can just be."

For a moment Angela looked offended, then she smiled with

compassion. "I feel sorry for teachers," she said. "Kids are so out of control."

Nan said she didn't think control was necessarily so all-important.

"What is?" Angela asked, breaking open a muffin and picking out the raisins to nibble one by one.

"How about being who you are?" Nan thought she saw a flicker of yielding. "It's hard to keep hiding what you really think and feel."

All at once there it was, what Nan was looking for, what she feared—Angela's eyes squeezed shut, her face got all pinched up, she shook her head slowly, then opened her eyes. "I hate English," she said, her voice trembling. "You've always got to write what they want you to write if you want a good grade."

Nan tried to give a good-natured laugh. "I've heard that often enough that I believe you, it must feel that way."

"No," Angela said fiercely. "It's not the way it feels, it's the way it is." Their eyes locked for a long blank moment, then Angela's face brightened as though she were remembering a miracle. "This guy I met, Kiser, says to write stuff like how it *feels* when your dad gets killed in a car accident, then they give you an A. He's already graduated so it's like he knows."

"But if your dad didn't—"

"Or you can make it cancer. Pisspot gave me an A-minus for a brain tumor. Kids call her that," she explained, her tone encouraging tolerance. "Her real name's Nesbitt or something."

"I suppose good writing is good writing," Nan said.

Angela's aggressive smile went blurry for a moment, as though she were testing that equation for insult. "I still hate it," she said, but not as loud. Her fingers sifted through the pile of muffin crumbs in her palm. "I mean writing that stuff just makes you feel guilty. What if it happens afterward in real life and you already wrote it, it's like maybe you made it happen." She glanced at Nan and scowled. When Nan thinks about Angela now that Will's gone, when her nerves flare at the prospect of seeing her again, she remembers that transparent scowl, the wishful, guilty child underneath.

That afternoon in early fall, Angela recovered quickly. "Kiser doesn't even know what his dad looks like, except for one picture," she told Nan, with a toss of the head. "Well, I did get a good grade. Maybe next time I'll do you. I'll even let you pick how you want to die."

If that was the first time Angela mentioned Kiser, Nan hardly noticed. If Angela began showing up with rusty blotches along her throat, if she seemed jumpy sometimes, sometimes a new sort of remote, if there was an interim report now and then from Kennedy High School, if there were scabbed initials knife-scratched on the insides of her arms, if Kiser was steadily insinuating his life into theirs, Will and Nan just didn't notice, absorbed as they were with what pranced before their minds' eyes—Angela on Brandy.

And then the Sunday after Angela's eighteenth birthday, Nan and Will drove out early to pick her up and she wasn't home, had never come home. All Nan remembers after that is Will frantic, Will furious, Will obsessed, Terri tranquilized but still oozing accusations. Trips to the police station, appointments with lawyers, psychiatrists. If you were going to get your daughter back, you ought to do it right.

Although they finally traced Angela to an apartment she and Kiser had rented in the northern reaches of the county, there was no legal way to budge her from it, or even get her to open its door. Nor was there any way to keep her from going back to it after she finally did show up at her father's house in the middle of a muggy August night, enormously pregnant, a bloody towel over a gap in her upper front teeth. She and Kiser were dancing, she said, and she tripped and fell against the wall.

The next day she gave birth to Megan Michele.

Two weeks later in a transaction that included Brandy, Will acquired Simone, a prize-winning Percheron draft horse the color of storm clouds, and her antique cart and harness trimmed with silver and red.

THE last time Nan saw Angela came as a surprise. It was Saturday morning and the girl barged in on Nan, riding Megan Michele on her back. Angela was wearing pink shorts with a bib front, a

T-shirt from Diggity's, where she waited tables, pink padded high-top sneakers, and a pink diagonal slash across each cheek. The baby was dressed all in pink to match.

"I didn't think you'd be here," she said to Nan, who might have told Angela the same thing.

Extending her arms in the direction of Megan Michele, Nan asked instead, "Where else would I be?"

Angela turned Nan the shoulder with the diaper bag then slid the baby around and down to the floor, where she draped herself over her mother's Reeboks. The back of her mother's T-shirt said, *We put the meat between the buns.* "I thought my dad said you guys had to go somewhere."

"He must have said *he* had to. He spends a lot of time with that new horse of his." They brushed looks. Angela had the advantage of mascara, liner and two shades of eyeshadow. "I guess I should be thankful that he's not trying to *ride* her," Nan said with a breezy laugh. "You could break your neck falling off a horse that size. But it's still awfully strange."

Megan Michele was rocking on her hands and knees. Both women gazed down at the wispy curls that fringed the back of her head. Then Nan heard herself saying, "You haven't seen his full beard, or the black frock coat and top hat. He looks like some turn-of-the-century undertaker, standing up there on his fancy cart, cracking his whip. He isn't really himself. At least I hope not?"

Angela shrugged, one side of her mouth drawn up in contempt. Nan had babbled again.

"He said it was OK if I used your phone," Angela said. Will had pleaded with his daughter to put in a phone. Finally she'd said she and Kiser had no cash for the deposit, and Will had given them a check. That was ages ago.

"Feel free," Nan said, then brightly, impulsively, she asked, "How's your new tooth?"

Angela's hand flew up to her mouth. She frowned—couldn't imagine why Nan should ask such a question—then she dropped into a squat. "Look at Megan Michele's," she said, wedging a finger between the baby's lips to reveal four white chips. Megan Michele tried to squirm away but Angela held her by the soft, indented nape of her neck, kept the glistening teeth exposed with her finger, looking up at Nan as if offering proof that all was not lost. "I don't guess I got any phone calls yet?"

"Calls here, Angela?"

"I put the truck in the paper," she announced rising. "With this number. Kiser keeps coming into the restaurant and going off on me. He says a truck should go to the man, and I get *her*." She budged the baby by lifting one foot. "Besides I'm tired of paying on it *and* the Visas."

The truck was a sky blue Silverado with a rollover bar and giant tires. Kiser had to have the truck. The check Will gave them to finance a wedding became the down payment. Kiser was on the stocky side with a snub nose and no apparent neck. Angela had to have him. He walked with a swagger, fell into bad moods, and quit jobs. Megan Michele was large for nine months, and though sticky in places and speckled with heat rash, apparently healthy. They had to have her. The way other babies smiled, she puckered her mouth into an O—an odd little reflex—maybe she was sucking in air to sooth her teething gums, maybe she was trying to say, *If you only knew what I've seen.* But what Nan wanted to know long looks at the child would never reveal: the depth of Kiser's imprint on her cells?

Such are the facts Nan assembles in her mind now, facts that should have made it impossible for Angela to say she was tired of anything. But they didn't, and she did. Kiser had left for bigger bucks on the Eastern Shore. The truck was up for sale. "It's over," was all Angela said that Saturday, and Nan flexed her clenched lips into a smile at the baby, then retreated to the kitchen to fix them some lunch.

How could Angela have known so definitely what she had to have, Nan wonders. How could she have done with such certainty and then undone without a trace of shame? It had taken Nan almost forty years to get up whatever it was you had to get up to get married. And always, whenever Nan had tried to compile reasons for bearing a child, her mind had gone blank. Almost forty years to do part of what Angela had done in eighteen, and Kiser twice in his twenty. As Will and Nan sat up through the night in the hospital waiting room while Angela labored with Megan Michele, Kiser had appeared with his mother, a woman with blue pouches under her eyes and thin hair that wouldn't stay in its rubber band. She'd drawn Nan aside and told her that Kiser's luck must be changing, praise the Lord, because he'd gone through all this before with another girl up in Mt. Airy, and the baby was born dead.

SEVEN years later Nan isn't ready to deal with Angela. She needs more time to compose herself, return to original intentions, let shame and sorrow settle into relief. She needs to understand first why desire wells up and then falters. Why one night in the dark her husband, whose decisiveness once captured her, convinced her to give up a life of sleeping alone, this husband left her side for the daybed in the den. Maybe it was because she looked grotesque at night, monkeylike, in a plastic mouth guard to keep her from grinding her teeth. Will never mentioned this, and she never asked, but then Will could never come right out and admit that Project Angela had failed either, even after Angela took off for the West Coast and, eventually, the change of address cards stopped coming. Just as Nan could never bring herself to complain about the amount of time he spent decorating and driving that horse.

And then one day, when she thought she had grown past caring, Nan awoke to the surprise of a man's touch, Will stretched beside her again, guiding her hand to where he was hard. It was like a silent dream, strangely impersonal. She suspected that it was the doing of the tape his minister had given him, *Self-Hypnosis and Sexuality,* which he was listening to behind closed doors, but such suspicions seemed trivial, she would not let them interfere. Nor did her hideous mouth guard, which she didn't even remove. Dreamlike, impersonal, it might never occur again.

But it did. Week after week. Until she suspected desire had succumbed to sheer assertion, pleasure to proof, and her suspicions began to interfere. One morning, when he was finished, his body rolled away from hers and his eyes went dark with surprise. He muttered something she could not make out and as she leaned across his chest to hear more clearly, his eyes looked far beyond her. She thought he said, "Give me a hand," and then he made a terrible face and his own hands closed and opened on air.

Nan has felt she needed to understand these things before she tried to find Angela. But Angela found her first.

COMING through the arrival gate from Phoenix, Angela is tinier than ever, in a short black dress, a maroon suede jacket with fringed arms, high-heeled cowboy boots, and a rhinestone in the flange of her nose. Marching a step ahead of her mother, a loaded backpack slung over one arm, Megan Michele looks large for her eight years, large and sturdy. She is wearing a baggy sweat shirt over a denim jumper and waffle-weave long johns under it to protect against December in the East. A bushy tail of hair spouts to one side and her forehead seems permanently flexed to entreat. The child stops in front of Nan; they exchange stares: *who are you?* each wants to ask.

"The spitting image of Kiser," Angela says, not proudly. The time for hugging each other, if they were going to hug, has passed. "Acts like him too, stubborn little know-it-all."

"No," Nan says. "I don't see any connection." The last she and Will heard, Kiser had landed where he belonged, in jail.

Angela rummages through the huge leather sack that hangs from her shoulder, pulls out a bronze-horse key ring, a broken comb, two white plastic bags, packed tight and knotted, a wad of charge receipts, finally a pack of cigarettes. "This is all the luggage we brought," she says, as she lights a cigarette then holds it down behind her back like a secret. "More like all the luggage we've got." There are brown spots on her teeth; tobacco stains or decay, she is not taking care of them. "I can't believe it's happened."

"That's totally normal," Megan Michele says, folding her arms across her waistless middle. "We had this unit in school on death and dying."

Angela takes a deep drag of smoke. "Can't we like see him one last time?"

Nan shakes her head. "If I'd known how to reach you, I—"

"Some people have to see the body," Megan Michele explains, the fat ponytail above her left ear bouncing with certainty.

"You'll just have to trust me," Nan says. "For once." Angela blows smoke over her shoulder. "One minute he was with me," Nan says. "The next minute he was gone."

"What about CPR?" Megan Michele asks with a slight whine once they are in the car. "We had this unit in school on CPR."

"My heavens," Nan says.

"Didn't you do it?" The girl has bounced forward to poke her round, sunburned face between the seats.

"Megan Michele, buckle up, it's the law," her mother says.

"I'm going to be a paramedic," Megan Michele says. "I like saving people. I sort of like seeing blood."

"Your grandfather had a massive stroke," Nan says, feeling suddenly old, the next in line.

Megan Michele flops into the corner of the backseat, out of sight. "You could still do CPR," she says.

WHAT is Nan going to do with them? Angela has taken over Nan's fisherman's sweater and the den, where she stays up half the night watching TV and filling the room with cigarette smoke. And every time Nan turns around, there is Megan Michele, who keeps bringing up the subject of CPR, her mouth puckering in remonstrance. When she isn't trying to stir up guilt, the child hovers in the kitchen, asking questions, opening the refrigerator, the oven, poking her blunt little nose into every bowl and pot—she doesn't really care for anything made from scratch, she explains. It's just that she's used to her own cooking, the tastes that come in boxes and foil packets and plastic trays you can put in a microwave.

Though it has been weeks since he died, Angela is obsessed with seeing her father one last time. She stares at the framed snapshots on the mantel—Will in a wet suit, Will with ten-foot wings strapped to his back, Will in gray pinstripes, standing beside Nan with her daffodils in that too-youthful cotton dress.

Angela used to accuse Nan of *getting heavy* on her, and why not

give her what she expects? "His spirit lives on in each of us," Nan
tells her. It's what Nan's own mother promised, her face all puffy
and alarmed like someone roused from sleep, when Nan's father
didn't survive his last binge. Nan never denied it aloud, never told
her mother no, no spirit that weak and sentimental was ever going
to live on in her—not in her mind, not through her body.

Angela takes down a five-by-eight of a black horse in profile,
its enormous size and strength mocked by the high, pointed collar, the patent-leather bridle and harness, all encrusted with fake
rubies and rhinestones, and the red ribbons woven into its mane
and binding its tail. At its rear is hitched a dark, silver-studded
chariot; facing the camera, legs planted apart, arms folded over his
chest, Will grins through a full gray-white beard. She holds the picture out to Nan.

"He had presence, your father," Nan says.

"So that's the horse?"

"Simone," Nan says with an attempt at gaiety. "I don't know
what he saw in her."

"Mid-life crisis," Angela says. "It wasn't his first."

"What are we going to do with her?" Another complicated
question. This gigantic creature whom Nan has resented when she
couldn't ignore—finally, she is in her hands. "It costs $300 a month
to board her. The cart and harness are worth thousands. He kept
adding things, getting fancier and fancier. He couldn't stop."

Angela just squints off through a puff of smoke.

Megan Michele plants herself in front of her mother. "Did you
ask her what's in his will yet?"

Angela yanks her daughter into a hug, presses the girl's face into
Nan's sweater. Bits of cigarette ash land on the child's head, more
drift down to the carpet.

"Will didn't leave a will," Nan says with a silly giggle. "I don't
think it ever occurred to him that he would die."

Angela buries her mouth in Megan Michele's hair. The two of
them begin rocking from side to side, sort of like disaster victims
waiting for relief, Nan thinks, or lost children. Maybe they are asking her to make a place for them. How can she, when all she wants
is her old life back, separate and whole?

"As far as I'm concerned," Nan says, "Simone belongs to you, Simone and everything that goes with her."

For the first time ever, Nan seems to have caught Angela by surprise. Megan Michele wrenches away from her mother's grip and contrives an upward slap of Nan's palm. Angela looks afraid.

"You could get a lot of money for her," Nan goes on. "Enough to buy another horse for you and maybe a pony for Megan Michele. I've wondered whether you ever miss—"

"Not," Angela says. "What good would it do for me to start missing stuff?"

"Even the three-hundred dollars a month. You could have that too. Till you got your feet on the ground."

Angela grimaces: how could Nan still be given to such dumb ideas? She begins rubbing her eyes until they appear to be melting down her cheeks.

"I think your father would have wanted you to have that much," Nan says.

Angela looks like someone about to jump from a high place, about to be forced to jump. "I don't want anything from him," she says, her voice cracking.

"Yes, she does," Megan Michele says, moving right under her mother's bowed head, looking up into her mother's face.

"Your father thought the world of you, Angela."

"Is that why he sold my horse?"

Yes, Nan thinks, but the word seems too complicated to speak.

"How could he just take it away"—Angela's closed eyes ooze darkness—"after he gave it?"

"He was angry. And hurt."

She pinches her face shut again, then relaxes it. "Well, maybe I am too."

"This is totally normal," says Megan Michele, patting the small of her mother's back.

"You stay out of it," her mother tells her.

Nan says, "He didn't know what to do."

"You think I did?" She throws Nan a look of such scorn that Nan has to remind herself that she, Angela, once seemed to know everything. "Why did he have to do anything?"

"That's a good question," Nan admits.

"It's sick, the way you try to understand everything," Angela says. "The way you're always trying to *communicate*."

Her conviction smothers Nan, the way conviction in other people always has. "You don't know me, Angela," Nan manages to gasp, but Angela is busy with a Kleenex, reshaping her eyes.

NAN will probably never know Angela. But Megan Michele keeps seeming familiar. Nan looks in on her in the guest room from the doorway, this mystery child who has sprung up between the crisp floral sheets, wearing one of Nan's flannel nightgowns, the sleeves rolled thick around each wrist, her hands clutching a book. Her loose hair is fanned on the pillow like a tangled headdress; her plump cheeks shine. Spread around her on the flowered comforter are other books from her backpack, some of the very books Nan loved as a girl. As Nan used to, Megan Michele has read them each four and five times. She's told Nan, "I like it better when I know what to expect."

Tonight she hitches herself up on one elbow and says, "My mom's upset, but she'll get over it. I mean, we need that money. That's what we came here for."

Nan nods. Does she wish the child were less honest, or that the situation were less simple—pay Angela off and she and Megan Michele will go away?

"What are you going to do with the money?" Nan asks.

Megan Michele shrugs herself back onto the pillow.

"What would you *like* to do with it?"

"I don't think we can go back where we were."

"But school will be starting up for you again soon."

"I sort of like school," Megan Michele says.

"Where do you think you'll go next?" Nan detests prying, yet she keeps on asking questions. It's as if she craves the sound of the girl's voice answering, slightly plaintive, but absolutely candid, like a memory that won't quite come clear.

"She doesn't tell me," Megan Michele says. "She sort of doesn't like having a plan."

"What would *you* like?" Nan asks again, prying, searching.

"To meet my dad."

Nan reaches for the doorjamb and takes a breath.

"Did you ever know my dad?"

Nan nods. "Not very well."

"Is he really a heartbreaker?"

Nan backs away from the threshold, puts a hand to her mouth, but doesn't blow a kiss. "You could probably call him that."

NOW that she has offered, it seems obvious to Nan that everything to do with Will's horse must be sold and the money returned to Angela, finally and unconditionally—no prying, no interference. Yet the next afternoon, as she drives mother and daughter out to the farm, doubt comes over her, as it always does.

They are all three bundled in Nan's clothes. Angela has belted the fisherman's cardigan like a kimono over her black, skin-tight stretch pants; Megan Michele wears an extra knee-length sweatshirt over her own. Nan leads them down the narrow passage beside Simone's empty stall, shows them the strips of silver bells, the whip, and the elaborate harness—a crisscross of patent-leather straps that bind the horse's dark strength to the wooden hitch and cart, which gather dust in another shed. When Nan tries to explain to Megan Michele how it all worked, this hobby that absorbed Will in his last years, the child just gazes at her skeptically, suspiciously, as though Nan must be making it up.

They catch up to Angela, who is already heading out toward the open, rolling fields. The horizon sinks and rises in front of them; the sky looks thick and gray. "Do you think it's going to snow?" Megan Michele asks. "I sort of like seeing snow, but I can't remember if I ever did."

Nan reaches for her cold bare fist and rubs it for a minute between her gloves before the child pulls away, runs ahead up a hill. The ground is frozen, lumpy, and Angela wobbles along in her high-heeled boots. Then from the crest the three of them spot a small herd of horses—mostly chestnuts, one paint, shaggy in their winter coats—and in their midst, Simone, huge and dark. Having gotten wind of humans, the horses pause in their grazing, heads raised, forelegs braced.

As Angela approaches the herd, it begins to drift along the fence, casually, carelessly, yet keeping constant the space between it and her. Simone seems to be coaching the others in this—to ignore the carrot, sugar, even their own names, because each is only prelude to the bit. After a few minutes of it, Angela halts. "All right, you guys," she shouts to the horses. "That's enough, goddamn it." She marches toward them again at as brisk a pace as her boots will allow.

They look away from her indifferently, but they slow their drift and she gains on them. She stops and screams at them again, and this time, when she starts toward them, they don't move. Then she shouts back, "What are you waiting for?" So Megan Michele and Nan advance, pretending indifference too.

Angela reaches the horses. Heads toss and snort. Muzzles poke at her, and she shoves each away with the heel of her hand, opening herself a trail into their center. They close ranks around her and she is lost. Megan Michele and Nan exchange a look of suppressed panic then stumble stiffly forward. The paint swivels away from the group and ambles out to meet them, nibbles around Nan's hips and up the arm of her jacket, turns and ambles back.

Soon they too are surrounded by restless shoulders, flanks, swishing tails. The air seems warmer, steamy with mingled breaths. Megan Michele is clutching Nan's hand and Nan is clutching back. "If we just stay calm," Nan tells her.

"I am calm," she says. Her cheeks are a raw red and she keeps sniffling. "I sort of like how they smell."

There is a shift of bodies, and Angela appears, her right arm stretched straight up so she can hang on to the noseband of Simone's halter. "Here she is," she says, yanking on the band, pulling the mare's head down from its great height until the muzzle rubs her cheek. With her free hand, she gropes in her shoulder bag and comes up with an offering of Rolaids. Simone's black lips part to reveal teeth as big as piano keys.

Megan Michele strokes Simone's velvet nose. Nan is thinking that the nostrils are just like the word sounds—large, open, sensitive. Nan is thinking how wary and lonely the eyes are, with their drooping lashes, each fated to its separate one-sided view. Nan is thinking so many crazy things—about insurance money, enough to buy a place in the country, and give it over to grazing horses, and maybe have Megan Michele come and live with her. They would never ride the horses, but only watch them and walk among them, and maybe somehow their presence would erase all trace of Kiser in the child.

Angela is saying that bareback is the only way to ride, the only way to become one with the horse. Her dad always tried to discourage it; said it set a bad precedent—a horse who wasn't too crazy about the girth or the bit might get the wrong idea, might think it had options. Besides Angela might hurt herself. But when her dad wasn't around, Angela used to forget the saddle and take off down the trails on Brandy, her hands full of mane.

"It's real easy," Angela says, "much easier than messing with reins and stirrups and stuff." When she tries to lead Simone closer to the fence, the mare jerks her head up, whinnying, and lifts Angela right off the ground.

Why doesn't Nan discourage this, not for Will's pragmatic reasons but for her own? Why, even when the darkening sky seems to drop down on them and a chilly wind starts? Maybe because she never feels she has a right to interfere, she is only a witness. Maybe because she sees they are made for each other, Megan Michele and the horse, created to some special, heroic scale.

Angela hands over the halter to Nan to hold—no more than she ever asked of Nan with Brandy. Then like a child herself, she scrambles up the slats of the fence, grabs at Simone's mane, and throws herself onto her. The mare seems not to even notice that someone is wiggling herself up to straddle her back. Now Megan Michele is crouched on the top slat of the fence with one hand gripping Nan's shoulder. Angela reaches, encourages, the child lunges for the curve of space in front of her mother. The horse shifts her hooves; her ears twitch. With all the authority she can muster, Nan gives the halter a firm tug.

Angela is offering directions—legs loose, hips loose, seat deep. "Pretend you're sinking in," she says. Megan Michele closes her eyes, puckers her mouth, sort of slouches down. Then Angela's boot kicks back, Simone takes a quick unbalancing step, and Megan Michele falls forward, clutching at mane.

"Don't fight the motion," Angela advises. "Roll with it."

Megan Michele rights herself and now her body absorbs the jolts and the three are off. Simone's walk is uneven, slow, but they are moving away from the rest of the herd, which starts to follow halfheartedly, then returns to cropping the meager grass. Megan Michele looks back at Nan her mouth in a wide-open smile, and jerks a thumbs up, which throws her off balance again. Angela, her gaze on the distance, doesn't seem to notice. *Sink in,* Nan whispers, as the child wobbles herself back into line, shoulders over hips.

Simone follows the fence, which angles off across the hilly field. As they climb the first rise, mother and daughter lean forward over the mane, and when they reach the crest and start down, they lean back toward the rump. Then comes another rise and then a slope that drops much deeper than the first, and they sink out of sight. When they appear again, it is not where Nan expected, but on the other side of a fence, farther away than seems possible.

That is when it does start snowing. Large, soft flakes drifting like paper ash. Though Megan Michele's cheer falls faint on Nan's ears, Simone must have heard it as a command to trot. Nan worries that the child will be shaken to pieces, but Megan Michele is a natural, bouncing there in her mother's embrace, rolling with her, both of them become one with the horse.

The snow is falling faster now, beginning to stick to hair and shoulders. Nan wishes she could slow the riders down, make them stop, make them wait for her, wait with her—across the hills she hears Angela laughing—but she can't, and by the time she calls out to them that it is getting late and they had better go home, they are too far away to hear, and the swirling snow has shrouded them, though it must melt around such heat as Simone's, who holds her dark ground against the billows of white.

Throwing Knives

Throwing Knives

ARCHIE Gannon wasn't my boyfriend, he wasn't even my friend, his name wasn't even Archie, but Richard, after his father. He just happened to live downstairs from us in Emerald Village, a ring of brand-new apartments in the middle of nowhere, a good hour from Monterey and anything that spelled Navy. Archie went to Catholic school on a short, white bus, so he didn't know about the problems at my school, the way they made fun of the gentle accent I had perfected in Florida and my thick cuffed socks.

To Archie I was the girl who had driven cross-country three times and up and down the East Coast. I had seen the Rocky Mountains and a live alligator not in the zoo, while he had never been anywhere that wasn't California besides the motel his parents stayed at in Vegas.

Half the apartments in Emerald Village were still empty, so we never saw any other kids our age except for the sister and brother who had to walk through Iceberg Court to get to their house, which was a wooden rancher with a tar-paper roof that went with the land before they developed it. All its paint was gone and its porch had fallen off, but when Mother saw it, she said, "I guess that's my place in the country. And I guess this is as close as I'm going to get, a second-floor apartment on the north forty. If we had one of those ground-floor patios, I could have planted sour grapes."

Sometimes the two kids rode up and down Romaine Way with their father in a rusty black pickup, sitting up in the high knob of its cab, eyes straight ahead. I told Archie they were gypsies because they had black hair and pointed chins, and they looked hungry and deceitful. I told him to stop and stare when they walked by, to show we weren't afraid of them and that we were sort of rich. I pointed at the patches on the boy's jeans and the way the girl's socks had slipped down into the heels of her shoes. The boy stole a sulky, downward look at us, but the girl just kept walking, as if she didn't even know we were there.

Once we saw them and the girl was carrying a brown paper sack full of something and the boy was trudging behind, but when they were about to pass me and Archie, the boy scurried up beside her and grabbed a fistful of her sweater. She twisted her mouth to his side and said, "Get your hand off me or I smack your butt," which made Archie and me both take a step back. Archie crossed himself and started pushing a whistle through his buck teeth.

They never showed up again after that. I wondered if maybe we'd scared them away. If so, I would be sorry. I only wanted them to know who was boss. Then one night at supper, Mother said out of the blue, "Well, there went my last chance. I'm condemned."

We thought she was talking about wearing maternity clothes again. Father patted her hand and said, "Angie, you look great."

"My country estate," she said. "Nailed shut. They were at it all day. I don't want you kids setting foot on that property," she added to me. "You never know what sort of hole you could find to fall into."

"What happened to the sister and brother?" I asked.

"What sister and brother?" she said.

"What happened to the man with the truck?"

"There's no truck there now," she said.

ARCHIE Gannon wasn't really my friend, he was just this boy my age who had never been anywhere, with a head that stuck way out in back and teeth that stuck out in front, but except for my little brother Charles, who still messed his diapers, he was the only kid around to take with me, and I needed someone to go with me, in case I fell down a hidden hole, when I set foot in the yard.

I warned Archie to test each step before he put his full weight on it, because the ground could cave in any minute under us. We picked our way over bottles and broken glass, used tires, and rain-swollen trash—a Cheerios box spilling mushy O's, a Wonder Bread wrapper, a jar from Marshmallow Fluff. And there were rags scattered in the mud which you could tell had been clothes—I saw buttons and the straps of a slip. Archie kept jerking himself around as if he thought someone besides me were following him. He kept drawing crosses in the air until I felt a little nervous myself.

"They must of left in a big hurry," Archie said. "Maybe someone was after them." That was what I was thinking, but I didn't want him saying it.

"Maybe the father got orders," I said.

Archie went around the corner of the house. "Maybe one of them never made it out," he called back. I slunk to where he was stirring a dark mound with a rusty iron bar. "Ashes," Archie said, like it was a big thing.

"So?"

"You know what that is?" He poked out something pale and porous, like a piece of rock. "Bone," Archie said.

"You don't know," I said.

"Maybe *human* bone," he said, making marble eyes to scare me.

"Don't boss," I said.

"Maybe a sacrifice—"

"They had a cook-out. They fixed pork chops."

"—to the Devil."

"I'm going home," I said.

"I'm going inside," Archie said at the exact same minute.

"It's condemned," I said. "That means the floor won't hold you, or the ceiling'll fall in."

He slipped the silly rock into his pocket and began to pry the boards off the door with his iron bar. There was no stopping him, though I hated the way he acted so great, hated his shiny, grinning teeth and bulgy eyes, as the fresh nails squeaked free. When I followed him across the threshold, I remembered all the houses we'd had to leave, my mother's angry packing, her fierce sweeping and scrubbing, and I saw strangers sneaking into our rooms after us anyway, opening the doors of our closets and cabinets, sniffing for dead fires.

ARCHIE Gannon was just this boy my age whose mother Rose got to be friends with mine. On the afternoons she didn't work in the beauty salon, Rose came upstairs and drank coffee in our apartment, and one Friday night she and Mr. Gannon invited my parents to the El Rancho. Father never said they shouldn't go, but in front of Mother he told me that he didn't really care for the Gannons, because Mr. Gannon drank too much and Rose had too sharp a tongue. But, he told me, the reason he'd asked the Navy to send him to school this time and not to sea was so he could keep an eye on Mother, and that was why he would go along with anything she wanted. Then Mother told me, "Your Father's getting to be such a snob. He's got career on the brain. But he always loosens up after a while."

The minute our parents pulled out of the court in Mr. Gannon's Impala, there was Archie at our apartment door, waving the silver and blue pocketknife he stole from the boarded house. We'd seen that knife at the same moment, the shiny hilt sticking out from under a black and white striped mattress, but Archie got to it first. I told him it was stealing to take it home, but there was no telling Archie anything that day. He said the brown marks on the mattress were blood. I remembered the girl's slow proud walk and how the word *butt* came so easily out of her mouth and my stomach sank.

"You're tampering with evidence, then," I said. "We should go to the police."

He seemed to like that idea, but it didn't take him long to forget all about it and settle down to gloat over his knife. Now he wanted to show me how he could throw it all sorts of ways and get it to land point down in the soft cork tile of our apartment floors.

It was a game he called mumblety-peg, and he told me I had to lock Charles in the back bedroom with his blanket while we played it, because it wouldn't be safe for a baby. Of course Archie played better than me. When I was still trying to get my kitchen knife to flip off a finger or wrist, he would already be dropping his from the rims of his ears. He'd gotten very bossy and he said it was against the rules to trade knives.

But Archie wasn't even a friend, so we got along, and anything was better than watching shows on TV in an apartment without grownups—*Dragnet* and *I, the Jury*. Even though I was old enough to know better, they made me nervous even when my parents were there.

Not that Mother ever had much sympathy when I tried to squeeze onto her couch cushion and hold her hand.

"Girls don't do that," she would say, locking her arms around Charles. Or when I pressed my face into the pillow of her upper arm, "I can't manage a Sarah Bernhardt," while Charles tried to tear off my nose.

And Father, regal in the wing chair Mother had just saved enough money to buy, said over and over, "It's only a movie, for Pete's sake. It isn't real."

BECAUSE Archie Gannon was just a boy I passed some time with throwing knives, he saw my body. It was another Friday night in late spring, the apartment was hot, and I wanted to go outside after supper, where it was cooler and still light, but when Father got home, Mother said, "I've got to get away from this apartment or I'll go crazy."

And Father said, "Now Angie, it's all in your mind."

And Mother snapped, "You're so right." She soft-boiled eggs for Charles and me and stepped into the shower.

I got out the crackers and peanut butter and made Charles a few sandwiches, then stacked one for myself that was so tall I couldn't fit it between my teeth. Mother came in wearing pink nylon underpants, where you could see the shadow in front, and in back, the line dividing her rear end. She wiped the cracker mush out of Charles's eyes, and as she lifted him down he patted one of her nipples with his sticky hands so she had to use my napkin to wipe it clean. In your own family you didn't have to wear clothes—I knew that. And once in Florida when she took me to the doctor at the Naval Station to be checked for pinworms, Mother warned me not to have false modesty there. "There is nothing to be afraid of," she said after the doctor told me to take off my pants and I didn't. "There is nothing shameful about the human body." Except in my case she was wrong. Mine harbored pinworms. "He is only a doctor," she reminded me later. "He doesn't see you as a person—just a body."

Archie Gannon was only a person who lived downstairs who saw me as a body.

I followed Mother into her and Father's bedroom and leaned against the new maple dresser while she anchored her bosom with a pink brassiere and slipped on a petticoat with lace, smoothing it over her swelling abdomen in front. She was humming a tune I didn't recognize. "Rose is teaching me to cha-cha," she whispered to Father, who was changing out of his uniform.

"I'd rather see a movie," he said. He had been learning Commie codes all day, until his brain buzzed, and now that Mother was wound up, he could be drained. In a family you had to take turns.

"Pooper," Mother said, and stuck out her lower lip. "A drive-in then." She waved the glass stopper from her bottle of Evening in Paris under his nose.

"You sure are glad to be leaving," I said to her in my flat voice.

She threw me that look I hated. It said, *Isn't it too bad—you need me more than I need you.* Then she touched the tip of the bottle to different places on her skin, finally to her first two fingers, which she slid into the fold between her breasts. One part of my mind turned away in disgust. Another part told me to lift the inside of my arm toward her. Before she put the stopper back in, she scraped it across the crease at my elbow. Then she pulled her rainbow-striped dress over her head and bent back slightly so Father could do the zipper from where he sat.

In the mirror I saw his hand stop at the waist and have to jerk a few times to get it past where she was starting to show. Then it was careful not to catch the metal teeth on her mole, which if punctured would never stop bleeding. When it reached the top, it tugged lightly at the neck so that she fell back laughing onto his lap. In the mirror their bodies folded together. I tried to slice them apart with my eyes. When Mother saw me watching, she acted serious again, pulled at the tightness in her dress, and came to stand at the dresser mirror, where she fluffed her yellow hair with a comb, her face set in a searching frown, as if she hardly recognized her own reflection, or didn't want to.

WHEN I stepped from a bath into the apartment without grown-ups, I decided to let the warm air dry me. In the tub I had lain back for a long time, trying to think about the missing girl, because that week they had torn down the boarded house and also because I'd promised never to forget her. There wasn't anyone to make the promise to, and I didn't know really what to think about when I remembered her, but that Friday I was trying, in a vague, nervous way, to picture what could have happened in that house, and trying not to notice how my body, except for a thimble pit of water at the navel, was as bald and flat as rolled biscuit dough.

Life wasn't fair. I climbed out of the tub, got Father's shaving brush, and stirred soap on my face into a slick lather. With its mild bristles, I tried to scrub smooth the rough skin on each side of my nose, which was too big, so what I saw in the medicine chest mirror was like a photograph snapped at close range. When the drying soap began to sting, I shaved it off with my nails, rinsed, and changed to Mother's mirror, where I practiced my heart-shaped face, sucking in my cheeks and pursing my lips. I greeted the buzz of the doorbell with Mother's disapproving frown. Then I went to answer it, even though I figured it was probably Archie. In the living room Charles had headed for a corner and was pushing his back into it, clutching his blanket, and shouting, "No, no."

And when I opened the door, Archie saw my body. I didn't

even remember I wasn't dressed, because Archie wasn't really anyone, just this person with a stolen knife who lived downstairs.
When Archie kept staring up and down my body was when I remembered with a cold shock.

He folded his arms across his Dodgers T-shirt, tucked a hand in
each armpit, and smiled his gummy smile. "What do *you* want?" I
demanded, as if it were all his fault, but he could only stand there
and smile, while the rims of his ears turned red. I tried to slide
casually out of sight into the wedge of space behind the door—pretend nothing was happening—but one of his eyes showed up in the
crack between the hinges. I stabbed a finger at the eye then kicked
the door closed and went to put on my shortie pjs.

That is all that happened. That is what Mother later called my
side of the story after Mrs. Gannon came upstairs on Monday afternoon for coffee. I got home from school and she was sprawled
in one dining-room chair, her bare, polished toes curled over the
seat of another. She was wearing frayed terry-cloth shorts, and the
white skin of her legs was wormy with blue veins. Mother always
said Rose Gannon was a beautiful woman. She had those high
cheekbones, that thick dark hair pulled back from a widow's peak,
and it was a shame about her legs. Once Mother asked Rose to
teach me how to file my fingernails. "She is getting to be that age,"
Mother said, "and it may stick better, coming from a pro."

"We were beginning to wonder when you'd be getting home,"
Mother said as I passed through the dining room and Rose
dropped her eyes. Since this was not a question, I didn't answer,
but tiptoed back into the bedroom to change into shorts. I was
busy puzzling over the kids in the lunchroom today, yelling that if
I saw Kay, I should sit next to her, then cracking up. Charles was
awake from his nap, smiling in a puddle of milk because he had
torn the nipples off his two bottles again. When I came out, Rose
pressed half a cigarette into her saucer with her pointed red nails
and said she had to go. The walls quivered when she let the metal
door to our apartment slam shut.

"Come here a minute," Mother said, and led me into the living
room, where she sat on one end of the couch, tucking her bare legs

under her. Mother was lucky. She was on her third baby and had only one bad vein, hidden behind her left knee. I perched on the couch at the opposite end.

"Mrs. Gannon brought me some bad news this afternoon," Mother said, running her fingers along her shiny calves. That was why they had looked so serious, I thought. Mr. Gannon had lost his job again, or someone had cancer.

"About you and Archie," she went on.

I thought, *She has noticed the chips and gouges in the floor of the front hall, she has seen Archie's knife, he has told her we set foot on the condemned property.* I tried to make my face look cheerful and curious.

"You did a cheap thing," Mother said.

Cheap I didn't understand at first. *Cheap* was the porch furniture in the living room which Mother was slowly replacing. But *cheap* was also the woman who lived alone in the next entry and tiptoed to the Emerald Village pool in high-heeled wedges and a two-piece bathing suit with nothing over it. Once I showed Archie how to draw her naked, sideview and front. When I remembered this, I remembered Archie's eye in the crack of the apartment door, and I knew what Mother meant. My lungs felt punctured. They couldn't hold any breath. I watched my fingers lace and unlace in my lap . . . the church, the steeple, open the door. . . .

It wasn't my fault, I wanted to tell her. And it was only Archie. But she had turned to look out the window behind us, her eyes squinting unfocused through the venetian blinds.

"It's probably my fault," she said, as if to herself. Then she added, "It looks like it's time we had a little talk about men and women."

I wanted to scream like Charles being locked in the bedroom, *No, no.* No, I didn't do a cheap thing. No, it didn't really happen. No, I can forget everything, we can all forget. But I hadn't the breath to make a voice.

Finally I said, "There is nothing shameful about the human body." My voice pleaded with her to remember this. Only this.

"Women do not expose themselves to men," she said uncertainly. Then, more firmly: "Except after they're married. And they want children . . ."

I wasn't really listening. A part of my mind said, *you do not need to hear this*. A part of my mind had already figured this out but decided to forget. Better to forget than to think about the hook and eye on their bedroom door, the look on Father's face when he said, "Your mother and I are going to lie down for a while." Like Archie's look when he beat me at mumblety-peg: *You lose*, it said, *you'll just have to pretend you don't care*. Like Mother's look when she came into my room in the dark and sat on my bed and said, "We're going to have a new baby," and wouldn't tell me when I asked, *Why? Why?*

Mother was finished talking, about men and women sleeping side by side, about men and women coming together, about men pushing themselves into the bodies of women, the babies that pushed themselves out. Her face was beginning to throw me that look.

I wished I didn't expose myself to Archie, because now I was exposed to everything.

That night I slept with my bathrobe over my pajamas even though it was stuffy and hot. Under the sheet and blanket, I secured my pillow across my chest in case someone should come through the dark with a knife, looking for me. When I finally fell asleep, I dreamed about a secret door in the back wall of our bedroom and instead of opening into the cheap woman's apartment in the next entry, it was an escape passage to the outside. I got out of bed quietly, so as not to wake Charles, and crawled down the dark passage toward the hazy light at the end. Where space opened into emerald green hills and azure sky, where the missing girl was waiting, in a gypsy dress of pink and chartreuse. Together we climbed a hill which turned into woods, and in the middle, there was a pool with mossy stones around it. Then we were swimming round and round in the water, until she turned into a golden fish, with a round, sucking mouth and round, black eyes. "Stay here where it is safe," I told her, and clawed my way up the slippery side. "I will be back to feed you." When I stood naked in the dry air, I woke up.

It was still dark, but the glow from a street light came through the venetian blinds and made bars on the wall beside my bed. The pillow had fallen to the floor and my pajamas were damp with sweat. I pushed away the covers and sat up. A short cry came from Charles's crib, as though someone had punched him in the stomach, and then the wet sound of him sucking on his thumb. Then her gypsy face came into focus behind my eyes, and it wore that look, and I heard her voice like the hum of a flung blade. *Someday,* it sang, *someday.*

Mother Tongue

W HEN I was eleven, we moved from Norfolk to Stockholm, Sweden, where my father was assigned to the naval attaché at the embassy. As always, he saw the positive side. This was another shot at normal family life, where the father came home from work every night, instead of every six months. I got to go to a fancy private school, with the embassy picking up the tab. And the whole business had to be a plus where promotion was concerned.

My mother hung on to her doubts, but that was the way she was with him, sternly balancing his enthusiasms. "She likes to burst my bubble," he told people, and never recognized the way her posture stiffened, as if some other, private victory were being sealed, every time she finally gave in. When the Navy shipped all our household goods to Liverpool, England, by accident, he laughed away her claims that she had told him so. "Things will iron out," he'd promised as she fumbled around in the chilly, empty house we'd rented and worried about the winter ahead.

My father and mother, Charles and I each had a cot with sheets and one worn blanket, courtesy of our landlord, who also lent us assorted plates, utensils, and jars. Georgie, the baby, slept in the biggest suitcase on his own bunched clothes. Our father fixed the hinges so that no matter how much Georgie wiggled in his sleep the lid couldn't drop and smother him.

L'Ecole Française Internationale was a four-story facade of reddish stone in the middle of the city which held special classes for the children of diplomats. It must have been clear to the Sisters from the start that my knowledge of French was limited to what I had learned in Norfolk from a Miss Lafave during a brief exposure to ballet. But they were unfathomable women, the Sisters, in their dark skirts and heavy black stockings, their faces drawn like long gray masks. No matter how poignantly I tried to present my ignorance, I could not move them to either compassion or anger. They simply expected me, from my first day and every night thereafter, to memorize whole pages in their language on the subject of *Mesopotamie, l'Esquimaux,* or *la famille Lebrun.* My failure also to memorize the correct pronunciation was simply a matter of fact, to be brought to the attention of the rest of the class. While I tried with humble eyes and posture to plead my good faith before old Madame Sibouet, she simply stared up at me over her spectacles and nibbled the inside of her lips while the room slowly filled with the sounds of derision.

I was afraid to mention these humiliations at home. Between the certainty of living together for a full year and our bare circumstances, both parents had gotten edgy, temperamental. I loved my father desperately. Very tall and thin, he had a narrow, bronze moustache at a time when such adornments were daring. He could be deployed on the other side of the world but he would see to it that bouquets of flowers were delivered to my mother and me on our birthdays: *Always, Frank,* promised the neatly printed card. *Always, Father.* When he was home, he was a limitless source of practical wisdom—how to bluff a large dog; how to extinguish different kinds of fires. During his weeks on shore, I used to stand behind his chair while he watched *The Cisco Kid* or *Dragnet* and scratch his head. Later when he was back on cruise, I tried to remember the smell of his scalp.

But his steady presence now was like living a story you knew would not end well. It meant always performing and waiting to hear the one thing you did wrong. "It's only a little thing," he'd say, "but those little things pile up." As if I didn't know, and he did, about the mistakes piling up, burying me at school.

He couldn't accept it when Mother kept to herself. "Relax," he instructed her. "If you would just relax," and I could feel her silence get brittle and unsafe. Then I had to work to protect it, fussing at Charles and Georgie lest their mischief and blind demands become the last straw, cause it to buckle, casting us all down into something worse than silence, the bitter currents of blame.

Yet no matter how careful we children were, Mother could always stare suddenly off over our heads and wonder, "How in god's name did I ever fall for this one?" We could be about to take our places on the floor, at the corners of a sheet spread with Saturday's lunch—hardbreads and *lingon* jelly, sweet butter and cheese, her favorite strong-smelling Port Salut. A wave of autumn sunlight could be streaming through the wide window and warming the bare wood around us. Georgie could manage not to kick over his jar of milk. And still she'd ask, "What in god's name am I doing here?" and drain the taste from everything.

Our father sat cross-legged, a knife in one hand, a wedge of Gouda in the other. "Caesar's armies marched on bread and cheese," he would announce, passing slabs around on the blade.

"The more I think about it," she went on, still with a distant, speculative look, "the more I think things were fine in Norfolk."

"You mean, without me," Father said.

I broke the corner off a piece of hardbread, tossed it in the air, and caught it on my tongue.

"I mean, where it wasn't impossible to cook a decent meal for the children. Where we had a table to eat at. Where they had beds to sleep in."

I threw another piece of bread over my head, arched and fell backward trying to capture it in my mouth.

"Where I had a place to sit."

"If you took an interest in something besides those frigging books," Father said. She was staying up late every night, propped in a corner of the living room, rereading, by the light of its tarnished fixture overhead, her books about countesses and queens.

"I had plenty of interests in Norfolk," she said, wrenching me upright by one arm. We had lived there a long time for us—almost two years in the same gray-shingled house. She had put in rose-bushes against its sunny south side, and in back, she'd unrolled a wire fence around a playhouse left by a much earlier tenant and filled it with six Rhode Island Red hens. Every day she poked around in their feathery litter for the bright surprise of an egg, free of cost. But she could never get them to relax enough to lay.

Charles was throwing crumbs of hardbread all over the sheet.

She smacked his arm and then turned to me. "Is this how you set an example?"

ON weekend afternoons, my father went off on long walks, along the lanes of the village and down to the horseshoe of shops on the shore of Lake Malaren. He invited me to go with him. He said we should meet our Swedish neighbors, but our Swedish neighbors did not believe in gratuitous meetings and preferred to watch us from behind parted lace curtains. For the return route we bought a bag of macaroons or, my father's favorite, a few pieces of marzi-pan. Sometimes we passed a knot of girls my age. "*Hej,*" they cried in unison, their knees flexing in the quick curtseys my father's age demanded. "*Hej,*" he called back, to my embarrassment, his mouth full of sweet, scooping up air with his hand. "Come here a sec. *Komm.*" He held out our open bag as bait. But they giggled and shied off. "The Swedes are a cold people," he told me.

One Saturday as we approached our house, each bracing to re-enter, a girl was standing on one of the stone posts that flanked the steps up into the yard. The sun low and at her back, she loomed above us, then spread her arms and jumped, scooting to where we stood in the road. "Welcome to Sweden," she said, as if it were the opening phrase of a song. She was too intent on pronouncing the *w*'s correctly to smile.

"*Tack,*" my father said, the word for *Thank you.* He could barely control his delight. "*Tack so mycket.*" Without taking his eyes off her, he ordered me, "Quick, go get the book," as though she were about to run away.

She was smaller than I, though her face made her two or three years older. It was thin and cheekless, with a wide thin mouth and dull teeth. The upper lip dipped very long at the center, like a flap over the lower, and gave her a wry expression, the expression of someone not about to escape, someone appraising the situation with an eye to moving in. What I wanted to do was disappear inside with my mother, but I dawdled back with my father's book.

He riffled through it and put a question together syllable by syllable.

The girl's face pinched and wrinkled with the effort to understand. "May I have a look?" she sang. Then her face slackened into a wry stare. "Oh, it is Pia Brandberg. My-name-is-Pia."

"*Tack.*" He said emphatically. "*Tack so mycket.*" He eked out another sentence from the book with "Cynthia" at the end.

"Cynthia," said Pia. The *th* drew her tongue out and back over that upper lip.

I glanced at her and made my mouth smile. I didn't like the lilt in her speech or the way her straight hair separated to show the rims of her ears.

"So much for the language barrier," Father boasted to me sidelong.

"In the future," Pia said, "you must ask like so: *Vad heter du?* What-are-you-called. It is the Swedish idiom." I gave her a look that said I had no fondness for idioms. "I shall teach you," she said. Her small eyes glittered with purpose.

ON a good day at school, no one paid any attention to me. Bad days left me in such despair I hardly knew who I was. What had happened to the opportunities my father had touted, to make friends from other lands? There was the Egyptian, Ada, a single black braid down her back as thick as my wrist, with an aloof beauty beyond her years; there was Tulla from Finland, whose round face and rough red cheeks seemed to promise friendliness; and Geeta from India, dark and thin, with a gooey red spot between her eyes. They had in common a language I could not seem to learn.

And then there was Wendy, the daughter of the American ambassador, who, according to school legend, had mastered French overnight, who found my struggle to remember which consonants not to pronounce entertaining. Mornings in the cloakroom before we donned the school smock, she showed off her frilled blouses and furry sweaters, each monogrammed with her initials. She wore a gold pin etched with *Wendy* and tortoise-shell barrettes shaped like *w*'s. For larger political reasons which I could never have grasped, the Sisters allowed her free and capricious play in the class. She was the one who shot my attempts at recitation with snickering rounds, until I gave in myself to spasms of anxious laughter. Sometimes these spilled into incontinence—*accidents* my mother called them with Georgie—and all I could do was pray that the knee-length smock would hide their traces. At home in secret I washed them away.

Maybe it was Wendy's ridicule at school that fueled the contempt I felt for Pia Brandberg. Afternoons and Saturdays, I dreaded the scratching at our door, and when I dragged it open, the elfin, unsmiling face announcing, "It is Pia."

Did she think I couldn't see that?

"The persistent Pia," my father called her affectionately. It was fine for him—to practice a few Swedish idioms and then pawn her off on me.

"What shall we do now?" she always asked, as if we had just accomplished something mutually satisfying, as if we faced an array of choices.

Nothing, I wanted to shout. *Just leave me alone.* She never showed up with anyone else; she'd never been among the girls Father and I passed on our walks, girls who now and then strolled by our house, chatting in steamy bursts, darting sidelong looks around the yard, still stirring my hopes. Their faces ruddy with the cold, they seemed to exude gregarious well-being. They must be trying to make contact, but the inevitable presence of Pia, spidery thin, homely Pia, was scaring them away.

"I can't come out now," I might say to her diplomatically.

"It doesn't matter," crooned Pia. "I shall wait." Then while I watched from the kitchen window, she scrambled up onto one of the stone pillars on which she'd first appeared to us, and arms spread to perfect her balance, leaped back and forth between the two like an angel guarding the gates.

She worked on teaching me a game that involved juggling balls off the wall of our garage—she was an expert juggler and could keep four going, interspersed with hand claps, knee slaps, and full turns. Half-hearted, I fumbled around with two balls, and even though she allowed me extra misses per turn, she did most of the juggling while I watched.

As darkness crept into the afternoons, she invented a form of hide-and-seek that didn't permit you actually to hide your entire body, but rather position it in such a way that in the deepening twilight it could be mistaken for something else—a shrub, a mound of rock. It was another game that guaranteed her advantage, for she could melt into the dusk with me standing practically beside her. I finally let my brother Charles play with us, so I wouldn't always be *it*. Often as I held myself still and breathless, arms angled from my body, maybe, like the branches of the hemlock beside me, I could hear the cries of other players, other games, carrying on the cold air from other yards, and I wondered at life's unfairness, that it offered me nothing more than one weird friend, my own kid brother, and the challenge of trying to pass for a tree.

By November, it was dark at three o'clock and still there came the scratching on the door and the announcement, "It is Pia."

"What shall we do now?" I sighed.

"A bloose," she said one afternoon. "We shall sew for you a bloose."

"A bloose?"

"I shall teach you. With a collar, like so. And a pocket, perhaps. Do you wish for pockets?"

"A blouse." I said. It had never occurred to me to wish for pockets or blouses. I didn't care about clothes. My mother discouraged it; she was in charge of figuring out what I needed, and more important, what we could afford. I had never expected that to include furry sweaters or monograms. Now when packages of coarsely woven long underwear showed up on my dresser, through no wish of mine, I assumed I was going to need them, and grotesque or not they would have to be worn.

"Quite right, a blouse," Pia said. "Shall you come, have a try?"

Unsettling proposition—*wish for something,* she was suggesting, and what's more, that something might be gotten for nothing. I could hear my mother's reproach. Trying to act as though my following her was a duty to friendship, no more, no less, I entered Pia's house for the first time.

It was down a block toward the village center, a large cottage whose faded blue paint hung from the wooden siding in wide shreds. Inside a single lamp gilded the layer of dust on a grand piano in the living room. Cobwebs filled in the legs of a carved wooden horse on the hearth in the kitchen and threaded the blue-and-white plates on a shelf above. A pure white cat rubbed my ankles. Pia's mother bustled aimlessly in a dark dress and baggy apron. Her hair was pulled back in a bun to display the same pointed face as Pia's. She seemed terribly grateful to see me with her daughter and insisted on serving us hot chocolate, with a dollop of whipped cream. The way my mother's set expression was an unfocused scowl, Pia's mother's was a smile, twitched into place several times a minute, turned almost to a simper by protruding eyeteeth.

Pia was fresh with her mother. I didn't need to know much Swedish to understand *None of your business,* or *See what I care.* It made me uneasy to hear her rudeness echo unpunished, and I tried to make up for it by meeting Fru Brandberg's bleached blue eyes as often as I could and returning her smiles, twitch for twitch. When she left the kitchen for a moment, Pia dragged me away from the table, into the hall and up a narrow staircase. "That was a revolting performance," she hissed over her shoulder. I didn't understand. Which of us did she mean?

The next thing I knew we were in Pia's room under the eaves, which seemed to contain everything. The sloping ceiling and walls were covered with maps, over which were tacked photos, postcards, labels, envelopes, signs. Feathers and dried flowers and pieces of colored glass dangled from threads at the one window.

Rugs overlapped on the floor; dolls and stuffed animals lay heaped on the bed. Dresser and desktop held stacks of assorted boxes and books. A bookcase on one wall had been converted by upright dividers into an elegant mansion for the smaller dolls. Pia had made all the furniture herself, from more boxes, papier-mâché, scraps of wood and fabric and yarn. There were wire chandeliers, crocheted rugs, framed pictures, bowls of fruit, tiny down pillows and quilts on each bed.

"So this is your room," I said emptily, when it seemed I had to say something. The last thing I wanted was for her to think I was comparing it to the one I had been assigned at home, a servant's cubicle on the first floor off the kitchen, while the rest of the family slept upstairs.

Pia went right to the kneehole of her desk and pulled out a basket and from it a pile of neatly folded remnants of cloth. "These are for you to choose," she said.

It was too much. "I should go home," I said.

"For the *blouse*," she said.

"I don't really need a blouse," I said. "Why don't we make *you* a blouse?" She always wore the same dull sweaters, the same rumpled gray ski pants.

"Do you wish flowers or no flowers?" She stared at me blankly. I let out a sigh. "Flowers."

"Like so?" She pulled a doll from the crowd on the bed, tidied it up, then held it in front of me. It was wearing a blouse of flowered print, with tiny buttons, a collar trimmed with lace, and pockets.

"Did you make this one?" I asked.

"I make everything," she said.

She lifted my arms away from my sides and began measuring me with her tape. Her quick, light touch caused me to flinch, but that she ignored. Soon she was unfolding the cloth on the floor and cutting through it with long, crunching shears. Then she sat down at the old machine on her desk and began rhythmically pressing the pedal with her foot while she tugged at the cloth above, her pursed face aging with concentration. I continued to stand there until I realized there was nothing else for me to do. With tentative relief, I let myself loll back on the bed among the dolls. I had had my fill at school of being taught the impossible. It also seemed to me that the less I had to do with the blouse, the greater its chances would be of becoming one, and my chances of deserving it. So she worked by the light of a green-shaded lamp, and I watched from the shadows, and sometimes her foot pumped slowly and other times it broke into a convulsive race, faster than the eye could see.

After a very short time, she stood up and pointed to the floor in front of her. I rose and let her spread out my arms again. She draped me with flowered fabric, smoothed it across the back, pulled it down in front, straightened the shoulders. It was a shapeless tunic at this stage.

"It's nice," I said politely, pleased to find its appeal no stronger. She slipped it off and showed me the side seam, the special way she had double-sewn it to enclose the rough edges. "That's nice too," I said, and I was feeling more relaxed, enough to kneel beside the bookcase and study the decoration of each compartment. Pia invited me to touch things, as I wished, but I kept my hands folded in my lap.

After another stint of pedaling she stopped, reached over, grabbed a handful of my sweater and said, "Take it off." I obeyed her the way my mother taught me to obey the doctor. Then Pia helped me slip the blouse on over my undershirt.

There was no mirror in that room, but from what I could see of my arms and front, I thought I must look very stylish. Two puffy sleeves had attached themselves to the tunic, sleeves that gathered in a ruffle at each cuff. I studied Pia's face for confirmation, but could learn nothing from the way she fussed at the fabric, lapping it closed in front, a fan of silver pins pressed between her lips. It was a little tight somewhere—across the back, or at the armholes—but this was a constraint I could live with. When she reached into her pants pocket and disclosed a handful of red plastic buttons shaped like hearts, another sigh escaped me. I saw myself in the cloak room at school, and Wendy silent with envy. Pia's stern expression never changed.

She snapped her fingers twice. "Give it me," she mumbled through pressed lips.

I peeled the blouse off and handed it to her. She sat down at the machine. Oddly contented, I lay back on the bed and drew a crocheted afghan around my bare shoulders. "Did you make this too?" I asked her, hugging it around myself. I felt oddly, blandly sociable.

"I make everything," she reminded me.

Again her foot rose and fell on the pedal, her deft hands guided the fabric under the pulsing needle, the machine chattered hypnotically. On the train home that afternoon, I had been working to memorize another passage from *Une jolie maison à la campagne*, home of the family Lebrun, and for some reason it returned now to my mind in perfectly pronounced cadences—the roof touched in all seasons by the sun, the balcony adorned by the red pompoms of a climbing rose, Madame Lebrun happily knitting on the *rez-de-chaussée*, while beside her a canary sang in its cage.

There came a pause in the rhythm of the machine. "Pia," I said, "Do you know how hard it is to speak French? I'm never going to learn."

"I suppose not," she replied without looking up.

"You don't?" I hadn't expected her to agree with me.

"It is not your mother tongue."

"I don't care what it is," I said. "It's dumb."

"Because you are at home in English." She began pumping at the pedal.

I thought about this for a while, found her certainty reassuring. "But you learned to speak English," I reminded her above the noise of the machine.

Her foot stopped. "But I am not at home," she said. "I try for many years, but I am not at home." She began pedaling again and fiddling with my blouse, and as I watched, I seemed to feel every tug and stroke of her hands on the cloth, as though it were part of my body, threaded with my nerves. She pinned and basted and clipped the collar, and my neck bristled at the touch. It was an unfamiliar sensation, but I wished it might never stop. Until Pia announced that it was time for me to go, I watched those hands avidly, but it was still not enough.

As I walked back to our house in the dark, I thought that it would be just like Pia to come calling for me tomorrow with her mind set on doing something else.

I NEVER did see my blouse again. I asked after it once or twice, knowing that it must exist somewhere, lacking only its heart-shaped buttons—I could have sewn them on myself. "That isn't necessary," Pia told me. "I must fix it," she said vaguely. I didn't really pursue the matter; in fact giving up the blouse was easy. After months of adjustments and resignations, losses in translation, what was one more?

The next day after school, I went straight from the train station in the village to Pia's and knocked on the door. No one answered. The window upstairs glowed dully. I was about to knock again when Pia's voice spoke up from the shadows, "I do not wish to be in that house." There was a woodstack at the far end of the porch and she was perched, chin to knees, upon it. She wore nothing over her usual sweater and pants. "It is quite intolerable," she said.

"You'll catch cold," I said.

"It doesn't matter." She slid down and stamped her feet.

"We could go to my house." I hoped she could see as clearly as I did what an empty prospect that was.

She shivered. "It always doesn't matter." She shouldered open the door. In the kitchen Fru Brandberg glanced up from where she stood clutching the sink. Her eyes and nose were swollen and red. I made myself look away, kept moving behind Pia, until the dim intricate warmth of her room surrounded me. I threw down my books, dropped my jacket, sank onto the foot of the bed with the relief of someone arriving, after long absence, home.

Something was bothering Pia. She paced the channel between bed and bookcase, stopped at the window, pulled on her long upper lip.

"What shall we do now?" I asked.

She began to draw in the steam on the glass—a square inside a circle, a circle inside that square, and so on, until things all ran together. As if this had given her an idea, she asked, "Do you wish to play with the dolls?" She was teasing me, I thought, for she reached over and picked from the pile behind me the one wearing the miniature of my blouse.

"Sure," I said, and accepted the others she tossed in my lap—a mother with cottony hair and an apron, a father in felt trousers, then, like an afterthought, the male twin of the girl in the blouse. I carried them to the bookcase, knelt, and began amenably to arrange them in the living room. Meanwhile, I assumed, Pia would begin working on my blouse. The mother doll, having acquired a tiny book from a basket, was bent into a striped satin chair to read. The father, who didn't bend, lay on the matching sofa, leaving the boy to play some boy's game on the floor along the back wall. I was deciding what room, what activity to assign the girl when Pia began pounding on the bookcase with her fist and shouting in Swedish.

It was a strange creature she clutched around the middle and shoved headfirst into my comfortable scene—a bald baby doll painted dark purple, swaddled in black cloth, and under its chubby rubber arm, the one prop Pia had not made, a miniature lead gun.

From its little mouth hole where a toy nipple could go were coming those loud incomprehensible commands.

"Pia," I said.

She snatched the girl from my hands and threw her into the living room, toppling a spool lamp and the mother in her chair. She snarled again in Swedish, then turned to me and said calmly, "Put up their hands."

I began to understand. I reached into the room for the father, half the size of the purple baby, and adjusted his arms. I was working on the mother when Pia's Swedish became soft and sibilant. She jerked her head in my direction then made the same sounds, by which I understood they were my lines, rather the mother's lines, so I tried to reproduce them. Then flatly, out of the side of her mouth, Pia translated: "Please, I have done nothing. Please do not shoot me right through the heart."

As the scene went on, the intruder forced mother, father, daughter to take off the meticulous clothes Pia had made for them and assume embarrassing positions on the round doily rug in the middle of the room. And I continued to repeat the lines Pia fed me in Swedish, mimicking every melodramatic inflection, curious to hear the English translations that came afterward in quick neutral asides. "Would you like to see a trick?" the girl asked. "I will do anything you wish, but please don't kill me." The father began to rage at the mother for not locking the door until the baby threatened to cut his fingers off. The mother tried at first to be polite, offering the baby food, and was pitched again onto the floor. "What have I done," she cried, her legs thrust straight into the air. "Oh what have I done?"

Before long I wasn't pretending the emotion, it rose up to meet the Swedish Pia pronounced for me as though I knew just what it meant. The more I understood the showdown in the bookcase, the more I forgot everything else. There came a point, and I could not say when, when the script became bilingual, though my English parts still came to me by surprise, like translations from another tongue. The girl muttered nasty insults behind the baby's back. The father threatened the baby impressively with the full power of the U.S. embassy, but was butted aside. From where he landed face down beside the couch, he demanded that his own life be taken to spare the rest. My eyes filled at the nobility of his intention. But the mother I was holding had other ideas. She sidled up to the baby and whispered in my voice, "Why don't you just take the girl instead? We don't need her. Take her and leave the rest of us alone."

It was a terrible thing to hear. For a few seconds I was stunned silent, waiting, I think, for some objection from the father, but he was not moved to speak. Then more to escape what I felt than to give it expression, I started to whimper. I was still holding the mother doll, and I pressed her to my chest like a hurt child. "Oh Pia," I cried, "no mother would ever say that." I rocked back and forth in distress. "No mother could."

My tears seemed to elate her. Her eyes grew bright and her chin jutted sharp as a trowel. She picked up the father and threw the girl down in his place, then poked at her with his foot, exploding with a string of Swedish. Breathing as if she had just come running from far away, she blurted the translation: "It doesn't matter what happens to this one. I shall never think of her as mine."

She looked at me expectantly. I studied the mother doll in my hand as though its shape and construction would tell me what to say. There was nothing left. When I glanced up, Pia was still looking at me. I felt slightly dizzy, seemed to be staring out of a deep cave. I returned to whimpering.

All this time the boy sat neglected against the back wall. Now I heard fumbling amid the furniture, and looked up to see the painted baby point the gun at the boy's head, and fire it throatily. The boy fell sideways and expired without a word.

Walking home in the dark, I felt sick to my stomach. What had happened? I thought of Pia's own words, "a revolting performance." I had spoken forbidden words, thoughts, I had cried, sunk to some unspeakable depth. I would be discovered, punished. I made a promise to the starless sky never to visit Pia's room again.

For three days I kept it, assuming all the while persistent Pia would come to call for me and manage cleverly to break me down. When she never did, the promise faded into the shadowy irrelevance of other guilty reflexes, like smiles for Fru Brandberg. By the end of the week, I was trudging to Pia's house, trying to look less like a sinner defying Hell than a martyr approaching the stake. Her front door opened before I could knock, and there she stood like fate, that sharp, hungry face, the pallid skin, urgent eyes. She raced up the stairs by twos, I went after with attempted dignity. She greeted me on her threshold with the dolls. Hating her, and myself, I accepted them from her trembling hands.

Where was the flowered blouse, with lace trim and heart-shaped buttons? It seldom entered my mind, caught up as I was in the purple baby's hypotheses of violence. At school, when Madame Sibouet was her most impassive or Wendy her most supercilious, I imagined the most satisfying reprisals in which they were stripped of their power and pretense, along with their clothes.

After school in Pia's room meanwhile, we worked to embellish our basic scene. We set matchstick fires in a glass ashtray and threatening the family with the same fate, threw their smaller furnishings into the flames. There was open warfare now among the family members, as each offered to strike a different bargain with the baby. In the end, Pia always took over and brought off the recurring finale when the baby announced to the boy, "Now you're going to get it," and he did.

It must have been my father, the sailor, who once told me that the farthest stars have burned themselves out by the time their beams prick our night sky. It may be the same with shared secrets— no matter how dazzling, how outrageous their shine, it is phantom light, its source exhausted once shown. As the weeks passed, the scenes Pia and I staged began to lose energy. There was a limit to the delinquent novelties our minds could come up with. As the passion subsided, the murderous baby seemed silly. We began watching, hearing ourselves, and each other. That first revulsion I had felt toward Pia and what we were doing returned unchecked.

I think Pia was having a similar reaction to me. Her lines grew stilted, began presenting themselves in carefully composed but listless English. One afternoon when I arrived at her house after school, Fru Brandberg opened the door and gave me to understand that Pia had gone to the Milk Central on an errand, and I felt relieved. The next two days I went straight home and as if for penance, memorized more attentively than ever before a long passage about winter *chez la famille Lebrun*—how the snow covered the earth and wove a light lace on the branches of the trees, how the boy Maurice made balls of it, and his sister Jeanne slid happily on the ice, while the blackbirds, that is to say ravens, flew about the house seeking something to eat, but found nothing.

My partnership with Pia might have ended then, with the dwindling of novelty and need. I was slowly getting the hang of French, Wendy was running out of insults, and our household goods arrived, no worse for their detour to Liverpool. But then one night, just as we were sitting down to dinner at our long-lost chrome-legged kitchen table, my mother happened to mention what she'd learned from the woman who lived behind us: two years before we arrived in Sweden, Pia's brother had killed himself—put a gun to his head, pulled the trigger, very messy. It was information passed from woman to woman by pantomime and sheer resolve, for neither spoke the other's language very well. Apparently Pia's mother had dreamt of a career as a concert pianist for her gifted son, while Pia's father, who sold vacuum cleaners, wanted his boy to become an engineer. The boy didn't want to become an engineer. Or a concert pianist. He wanted to go to America and play jazz. His mother cried, his father laughed. So. My mother pointed at her temple. "Please pass the meatloaf," she said.

My stomach was churning. Spread in front of me were our familiar Melmac plates, the smelly old aluminum glasses from Grandma, the hen saltshaker, the rooster peppermill. Georgie was where he belonged, in the wooden high chair, scrubbed almost paintless. The rooms beyond had filled up with more familiar things—there were scratches on the coffee table and one leg of Mother's Ethan Allen sofa had been cracked, but, as though he were the expert, my father said the place had begun to look like home. Then how could this, what my mother said, be true?

"Apparently Mr. Brandberg went north after it happened. He chops down trees. His wife gets a little money every month."

There was a tinted sepia portrait of Pia's brother sitting on a square of yellow lace on the Brandberg's grand piano. I remembered the close-set eyes, their brown stare mocked by too-pink lips and cheeks. Pia had said he didn't live with them anymore. Her mother had nodded, twitching smiles. There had been no sign of a father anywhere.

"We should all of us try to be nice to Pia," my mother said.

I could feel myself flush under her gaze. Why was she looking at me? I didn't shoot Pia's brother. How could she dare pretend to look sad over this death of someone she didn't know? "Two hands," I reminded Georgie, who was raising his cup of milk.

"Cynthia," my mother said, as though she had an inkling of the games Pia had taught me.

"I *am* nice to her," I said. The fact was Pia was too imperious and preoccupied to notice whether you were nice to her or not. But what did my mother know? This wasn't one of her romances, long ago, picturesque.

"Does she ever mention?" my mother asked.

"Angie," my father said.

"I'm only curious," she said.

"I don't think it's any of your business," I said haughtily. I would defend my friend Pia, juggler, hider, maker, destroyer, from her easy words.

"Cynthia," my father said.

"You would think that poor child would have mentioned it." My mother's tone implied I was withholding information. "The poor child has lost more than a brother, after all."

In my mind I saw Pia in her kitchen, picking at her dinner, separated from her inconsolable mother by two empty chairs. I looked across at Georgie, who had gone red-faced and Buddha-like the way he did when he was doing his business; then at Charles, chewing potatoes and beets with his mouth open. Hadn't I known for some time the story my mother had just reported with such self-importance, maybe not the surface details, but the same dark, furious core? Tomorrow afternoon, I would call for Pia, we would turn our backs on these tables, these intolerable houses, we would walk the dark road out of the village arm and arm.

"Still waters run deep," my mother said. If that was supposed to be some wise reference to Pia, who talked and moved incessantly, she couldn't have been farther off.

"Dow," said Charles, pointing two fingers at the side of his head. "Dow, dow, dow."

She turned on him ferociously. "Don't ever let me see you," she said, slapping his hand out of the air. Charles tucked his fist in his armpit and laughed.

Outbound

WINTER came early in Sweden, catching us off guard, winter and the shrinking of day. Mornings were states of emergency, all of us huddled against the dark in the yellow-gray chill of the kitchen, speaking only when necessary: Mother wrapped in Father's bathrobe as well as her own; Charles and Georgie dozing over their cereal bowls; Father and I diligently chewing, tuned to the ticking of his watch.

At some precise moment, he went for his black muffler, crossed it carefully over his chest, slipped on his long black coat, pulled on gloves. He paused on the open threshold to position his gold-trimmed hat, then shouldered his way out through the dead cold to the car, with me struggling to stay in his wake. The heater would have just begun to work when we arrived in the village of Alsten, and he leaned across me and opened the car door. "Parting is such sweet sorrow," he always said, his mustache on my cheek. Then he drove off to the embassy, and I climbed the wooden platform to wait for my train.

Though both parents believed otherwise, I had not yet adjusted to L'Ecole Française or the long ride to and from it. The only child on the train, I hunched back into the hood of my coat and pretended to review the dim pages Madame Sibouet had decreed I learn "by 'art,'" strings of French words I could barely pronounce, but would be asked to recite at wretched intervals during the day while Wendy led the Marcias in coughing and the clearing of throats. Wendy, the living legend, had mastered fluent French in one hour; Wendy inhabited a house in the fancy Djurgarden with a swimming pool in the basement; Wendy dazzled the Sisters into overlooking her small violences. Because Wendy was the ambassador's daughter, I didn't dare worry my father with complaints, but with my mother, who despised the conventions of rank, I had tested an offhand report—Wendy had a tendency to spit through the gap in her front teeth onto my papers; her deputies, both named Marcia, made fun of my clothes.

Mother was not one for either sympathy or strategy; she taught the power of scorn. "I'd die before I'd let you behave like that," she said of Wendy. "I mean, spoiled rotten. And how two different women could pick the same wishy-washy name for their daughters, I can't imagine. At least your clothes are clean," she added, though I had not implied the other girls' weren't.

UP the escalator from the underground terminal, out onto the loud, slushy avenue of lighted signs and windows. A right turn at the Konditori, through the cruel fragrance of yeast and cinnamon. Then the short dark street, jammed with old snow and delivery trucks, and the hundred and four stone steps at its dead end, their heights lost in gloom, even when gained. There were different ways to take those steps—methodically, pretending they were no different from flat pavement, or by twos until your first energy flagged and after that with a suicidal will.

On the shopless cross street above stood the school, one in a row of blank facades. Behind it, a courtyard of fine black gravel had been pieced from the flat adjacent roofs on the lower block. Facing the school, fenced with wrought iron, was a sort of municipal park, the contours of a round stone chapel visible in its midst—all pretty substantial to be propped up there somehow above the *real* street, where the trains came and went, the avenue of escape, vaporous and glowing, each doomed morning disappearing below.

On the days I decided to get lost, it was always from the stone steps that I made my departure, their descent, a breathless flight — pure, unblinking motion that seemed so easy I wondered why my kneecaps trembled as I staggered away from the base, and whether the tears that welled in my eyes were what was meant by *crying for joy.*

MOTHER would much rather have stayed in Norfolk where there was a good long growing season for roses. She wasn't the one who'd joined the Navy, she'd said, and besides, for every minute Father was home, he'd been away four, so what difference was one more year going to make?

"It will broaden us all," Father had said. Breakfast was over. He was sitting at attention in nothing but his boxer shorts, trying to bite at a nail and hold Georgie on his thigh at the same time. He always came back from cruise with beautiful hands, but after a month of shore duty, each nail would be worried into its bed.

"I don't need to get any broader," she replied. One thing Mother did talk about was her thinness before bearing us three children and the mysterious futility of her efforts ever since to reduce. During Father's last cruise she had bought a special caramel, two of which before each meal were to dampen her appetite. She chewed four and five and six with increasing hunger, went through several boxes before the craving subsided. Just before he returned, she dyed her hair.

"This is one of those times," Father had finally said, "when we have to think of my career." We were to consider Stockholm a step up, he'd told us — he was to learn diplomacy.

"You'd have a better shot at dog-sledding," said Mother, washing dishes as though she hoped to break something. "They ought to send you to the North Pole." Then she asked, "What about schools? Cynthia's made friends at Herndon Junior." An afterthought, turning to me: "Haven't you?"

"How many times has she said she wanted to come to sea with me?" He ran his fingers across the table and pinched my ribs. "See a whole new country, Cynthia, learn a different language?"

All morning it seemed they argued about the move overseas by arguing about my welfare and what I was supposed to grow into, she sounding more and more disgusted, he remaining certain and calm. I must have understood that what they wanted from me was silence, for I remember having no preference in the matter. The tension between them had absorbed me, become me, to the point that I didn't ask myself, was unaware of a self to ask, what I wanted. Instead I waited to see which of them would prevail.

My father offered novelty, adventure. There were times, too, when I felt I had to shower someone with kisses and embraces. Father seemed to understand these rushes of energy, sat like an awkward statue, a hand on each knee, and received. When the frenzy had begun to subside, he might ask with exaggerated formality, "And to what do I owe this sudden display of affection?" My mother shrank from my touch.

But she was home: she filled our rooms with her breath, her smell, the current of her defiance. I remember a night when the boys were in bed and I sat up late in Father's wing chair copying a report on meteorites. On the sofa opposite, she was reading one of her books about historical romance. Under the lamp, the auburn rinse made her hair seem about to crackle and dance. I knew better than to interrupt, but I couldn't stop looking at her. After a while, she glanced up, not exactly at me, but as if a missing page were inscribed on the air between us. It must have been midnight by the time she finally said, "You know, I always expected it would be like this."

But that morning, with Father there in the muggy kitchen, she had cried abruptly, "What kind of life is this anyway?"

"Did I ever promise it would be different?" he'd asked. "Did I ever lead you to believe? What do other wives do? Was I supposed to know you were"—he paused out of a respect he always had for the perfect word—"antisocial?"

When I was younger, my mother had gone to her first and last meeting of Officers' Wives. My father had arranged for another wife to pick her up. My mother'd had to force herself outside to greet the carful of strange women, only to realize they were all wearing the hats and gloves she'd forgotten about, which had been prescribed in the special book Father brought home during his first week at OCS. Packed and unpacked countless times afterward, shelved with Father's *Atlas,* his college yearbook, the *Reader's Digest Manual of Home Maintenance* she gave him that first Christmas he wasn't at sea, the book was called *Smooth Sailin'.* On the cover was a photograph of a man in uniform, his arm draped with casual affection around a woman in a crisp white blouse. Her blond hair rose in the breeze. They were smiling and half-squinting at something they both could see on a lofty horizon.

"I have better things to do," Mother decided afterward, and that became one of her refrains. She began to fight in every way she could for a life apart—but I don't think it was the kind of liberation women seek now—it was a life without Father, without anybody, without noise and without hope, except the one she never acknowledged, that he would wear her down in defeat.

When she finally gave in on Sweden, her single condition was her perennial one—that we live as far away as possible from the people with whom Father worked. She was convinced she would hate diplomats, that they were dishonest and lazy. "You go ahead and be as attached as you like," she told him. "Leave me out of it." And she picked a house to rent in a village suburb so remote that all Stockholm rose and spread its business between us and the American embassy.

It was a stucco bungalow the color of sand with green peeling shutters the landlord promised to repaint but never did. The backyard was one giant rock, slab on gnarled slab, lichen and moss growing in its creases. For days after we moved in, I would come upon her gazing out the wide back window. I saw nothing but the shabby fence. "I like rock," she said once, as though admitting something important. "More than the waves at Virginia Beach, or fire."

There were only the two bedrooms upstairs in that house, and

Georgie still cried in the night and Charles had to be awakened and taken to the bathroom. With great solemnity, Father pronounced my twelve years mature enough to be assigned the extra room on the first floor off the kitchen. Every night I felt like a decoy, the imitation daughter supposed to distract an intruder long enough for the real family to get away.

MAYBE my mother never wanted to be understood. Maybe she liked my father calling her *an enigma,* and all those other inarguable words. It may have been a sort of guessing game they played; if so, she didn't drop many clues. Father insisted she was smarter than he was, even though he had finished college and she hadn't. When he was trying to persuade her to attend some embassy function with him, he'd insist that *she* was the *conversationalist*—as if there could be only one of those in a family. "You should see her draw out a perfect stranger at a party," he'd say to me, in front of her. "When she makes an effort," he said.

Around the house she kept silent. Her housekeeping was inconspicuous, but efficient. She cooked sensible meals with sensible desserts like prune whip and angel cake. Somehow she made it clear that she couldn't care less about these accomplishments we might have admired her for. And they left her plenty of time to sit and read—or rather sit and stare at the ceiling or out the back window with a book in her lap. She defended her silence with a ferocity my brothers and I learned not to provoke. When I broached the subject of my daily failures with the Sisters at L'Ecole Française (as the smartest in the family, she might have had some advice), she told me, "This whole thing was your father's idea, talk to him."

"There's nothing to worry about," Father called from across the room, without looking up from yesterday's *Herald Tribune*. "Those French gals know where your tuition comes from."

Then smartest or not, Mother began to get sick. At first when she stopped eating, we thought she was reducing again and when she didn't comb her hair, we thought she had invented the odd style to conceal her ashen roots. But she was going back to bed every morning once Father and I plunged into the dark, and according to

Charles and Georgie, who quivered with the insult, she was closing her bedroom door. Father dosed us with the word *influenza* as if it would itself cure everything.

One day after school I found Georgie and Charles lying on the landing outside her closed room surrounded by all their toys, like supplicants in front of a darkened altar. They were still in their pajamas, and Georgie's diaper stank.

"We're playing this game," Charles said when he noticed me. "We're in the water."

Georgie slapped and kicked at the mess around him to suggest swimming.

"I'm Father," Charles said.

"I'm Charles," said Georgie.

"Someone put a bomb on the ship," Charles said.

Georgie made an explosive noise.

"Boys, please," the voice begged from behind the door, and then there was coughing.

Both boys looked at me then, full of questions. Did I see how it was to be left home with her? What did it all mean?

"Pretend I'm a raft," I whispered, lowering myself, swishing aside the spill of trucks and animals and blocks, and stretching out on the floor. "Grab a hand and I'll pull you on board."

BUT she stopped getting up at all, and we started running out of clean clothes and different things to eat. There was cereal for breakfast and cereal for supper, and because it was always dark, and Mother was always in bed, and there was nothing to look forward to after either meal, it was easy to lose track of where you were.

Her absence from the rooms downstairs was like a thinning of the air. You had to remember to breathe more deeply and got dizzy anyway. I began to imagine glimpses of her at the kitchen table, on the sofa in the living room beside the window. My jaws ached to see her anywhere but in bed—a heaving of blankets, a grimace of blue gray features—to do something more for her than furtively touch the ridge of her foot.

On the tenth day Father hired Agneta to iron his shirts, and she made cinnamon buns for breakfast. Then one afternoon when

I came in from school, Father was already home, upstairs, and with him another man, leaning over the bed. I had tiptoed to the open doorway and saw my mother propped on pillows, and the floor lamp dragged close to shine right in her eyes. They were shut, and her features pinched into a frown. She seemed to be trying to twist herself from side to side, but all she could manage to turn was her closed face. Her nightgown had been unbuttoned to the waist, exposing her breasts to both men. The stranger pressed a stethoscope into their softness, shoving each nipple to one side and then the other.

· I couldn't see enough of this, and yet I hated what I saw. My own body seemed to have rushed back into hers, still it stood on the threshold, growing faint with strange stirrings, as when Father drove us too fast over a rise in the road.

"Deep bress," the doctor kept saying coldly. "It must be done. Deep bress." And I imagined that he had opened our chest and was prodding our stubborn, shiny heart.

Father watched for a moment and then looked away, watched, then looked away, as though trying to conceal a longing. He turned his face too far, and our eyes met in the shadows. His pale skin darkened. My hand went to my own tender chest, to ward off the icy pressure against my own ribs.

"Close the door after you," he said.

I didn't move.

He stepped between me and what I could see of her. The spell broke. "She's going to be all right," he said. "The doctor is just checking for pneumonia." He pronounced the possibility with care.

"Is that Cynthia?" I heard my mother ask.

"She's going to wait outside."

"My God, Cynthia, I can't breathe."

Father still stood between us. The doctor prepared a needle.

"Young lady," Father said.

"I'm going to pass out," my mother called.

I backed away.

"I'll pass out."

"What means pass out?" the doctor asked.

After I closed the door, I heard her moan, but I knew of no

sound to make in response. I had never seen her like that before. I flung my body against the door and let it slide to the floor. After not so long, Father asked me to move out of the way so he could show the doctor downstairs.

"THIS roaming of yours," Father called it. He was waiting at the kitchen table when I stumbled in and flicked on the light. "What are we going to do about it?"

I had missed supper for the third time. Still convalescing, Mother had already gone back to bed; otherwise, she would have had something to say, a predictable repertoire of complaints: Did I think I could just come and go as I pleased? Did I think I lived in a hotel? "Look at your hands, look at your tights, tie your shoelaces," she would have concluded, and then forgotten the whole matter.

Father constructed cases and saw them through to solution. He was rational and wanted me to be. But what could possibly be rational about wandering around the city in the dark until my fingers and feet from the ankles down were frozen stiff?

"Wendy started it," I said, hoping my reference to the celebrated daughter would divert him. At the same time, I was ready to elaborate its particle of truth: two weeks before, in Ancient History, Wendy had snatched my Moroccan leather change purse. "Does she do this sort of thing often?" Father wanted to know, and I told him, "Yes, and mostly to me, because we're not supposed to pronounce the *st* in *est,* and I keep forgetting."

Since Madame Sibouet had not yet hobbled in, the Marcias had taken up positions in corners of the room and passed the purse like a beanbag, while I somewhat mechanically tried to chase it down. When it came around to Wendy the second time, she unzipped it and shook my coins into her hand. Someone grabbed my elbows from behind, someone else helped her shove one of the swollen windows up a few inches, and by the time we heard Madame's grating voice calling us to order from down the hall, my train fare had been flung out across the twilit street and into the hedges of the park opposite.

Madame was well into the lesson on the subjunctive by the time she appeared in the doorway, clutched the jamb, and stepped high and carefully over the slight unevenness at the threshold. Her brown wig had settled as usual low on her forehead, leaving a band of gray wisps at her nape. We were all at our tables, hands folded before us in the way she deemed crucial for our education. I had my empty purse back, and, I told Father, "That was what really mattered because it was a present from you. But," I added, "I had to walk home."

"It must be ten miles," Father said. "You could have called someone, borrowed money."

I shrugged stupidly.

All the other times I'd been late, he wanted to know, had Wendy taken my money also? I think he was bothered that I was not more actively cultivating her approval. "Oh no," I assured him. "That happened just once."

I turned away from him then and intending to show that there was nothing further to say or do except resume normal routine, started to fix myself a bowl of cereal.

"What we should probably do is take away your supper tonight altogether," he said.

The surprise of it stung me. I shoved the bowl to the back of the counter and made for my room.

"I don't mean that's what we will do," he said, stopping me by the back of my sweater.

I folded my arms, wouldn't look at him.

"You know, you could try harder to pronounce the words correctly," he said.

I was still feeling the denial of food. My eyes began to smart.

He sat me down at the table then, and told me it was all right, and put the cereal in front of me. "It's tough on you, isn't it?" he asked, and I had to clench everything not to cry. "The language barrier," was all I heard him say after that, for my mind grabbed the phrase and clung to it, repeated it over and over as if the words themselves would give me strength.

After a while he dipped up a spoonful of soggy flakes, and I swallowed it along with the staunched tears. "How about if you just start coming home right after school," Father said. It didn't seem like a question, so I didn't have to respond.

He stood up and circled the table. He put one hand in the high cupboard, reaching for his bag of American cookies. Mother paid an arm and a leg for them at the commissary and never let me or the boys have any. There were two left. "What do you say?" he asked as he threw one to me. I put it beside my empty bowl. "Why not?"

How could I tell him what a relief it had been that first afternoon to realize I was penniless and miles from home? I sat watching Wendy raise her hand with all the answers, and her smug voice had faded out and all I could hear was the tapping of Madame's teeth. And all I could think was that I had no choice but to strike out alone into the dark and the cold. No matter what would happen, I had no choice. After so many weeks of dull misery, I suddenly wasn't miserable at all. I wasn't even afraid, but rather amazed, that here was a thing I would never have even dreamed of, and I was about to do it.

I remember dressing carefully against the elements, leaving my *tablier* on for extra warmth. And I remember I almost ran at first, confident in the rush of my own blood, until the layers of cotton and wool were oily with sweat. When I slowed, the clothes turned cold against my skin and I shivered. *It's only cold,* I told myself, and refused to shiver again. When my legs became only tired, I pretended they were not attached to me.

The smell of hot sausages and mustard from steaming corner carts made me only hungry, enough to want to bite the air. But I wondered who had decided that smells just teased and couldn't satisfy? Why couldn't I change that if I wanted to? I was hardly aware that offices and stores had given way to modest apartment buildings; my eyes kept searching ahead for the tourist maps that stood at certain intersections in lighted cases. I pored over their weave of pinkish streets, the blotches of green, as if I could draw the whole city into my brain. From map to map, I plotted my return. Four hours after I had raced over the brink of those stone steps, I was sitting in the kitchen while Agneta heated the milk for hot chocolate.

Could Father really understand? I was poised again at the top of the steps.

"What about your own roaming?" I asked him.

He coughed a sharp laugh. "Touché." He got up again to forage for more food. "Maybe it's in our blood."

Maybe it was—a desire for home so intense that the only safety was denial and delay. I munched Father's cookie.

"I've been thinking," he went on. "Maybe this assignment wasn't such a good idea. Especially for the others." He stopped opening cupboards and looked at me, a request. "No. It's been tough on everyone. I don't know. I thought . . ."

"But she's getting better now," I said.

"I just thought," he said. "I just hoped maybe things would change."

"It's this game I play," I told him.

"It's your mother," he said, trying to make his voice sound jocular. "It's what they say—you can't live with her and you can't live without her."

"My game has two parts," I said. Then I tried to explain how the object of the first part was to get lost, to head down any street you felt the urge to, choices based on nothing but buried belief. If you had a little extra money, you got on a bus and got off anywhere. And the object of the second part was will power, finding your way to one glowing tourist map after another, finding yourself on each them, and finally finding your way home.

He seemed to consider these rules, shoving soda crackers into his mouth that I knew were stale. Some crumbs flecked his moustache. "Maybe that's what I like about sea duty too, you know?" His voice was different, lighter. I nodded. "Don't get me wrong," he said, "but I've always thought outbound was the best part."

Welcome Advance

*I*N less than a week after I showed my mother the bed of iris she chopped half of them down. She must have been holding dozens in her arms, cradled like a new baby, as she came around the side of the house and climbed the rotting steps to the back door. Her look defied me to ask questions. But I was twelve, and parental hypocrisy too delicious. I left my treasured American comic books on the blanket I'd spread in the yard and followed her into the kitchen.

"I thought you said," I said. I was thinking of the time back in Norfolk when Charles picked all the blossoms off her Peace rose, carefully, right below each flower to avoid the thorns. She filled cereal bowls with water and floated the peach-yellow blooms on their surface and stared at them mournfully all through dinner. If one of us children made a noise, she snapped, "How would you like it if someone pinched *your* head off?"

"These are for a centerpiece," she interrupted now, a refinement of the rules. "We're entertaining tonight, I told you. And don't go littering up the yard, either." She pronounced *centerpiece* and *enter-*

taining with such authority you might never guess that entertain was what she'd made my father swear never to ask her to do when the Navy assigned him to the embassy in Stockholm, if he wanted her to go with him. She said she wasn't going to play up to anyone, and she didn't want anyone playing up to her.

"I thought you said," I began again. I was thinking of her indifference just last week when I dragged her downstairs and outside to see the miraculous iris in the first place. "There's nothing special about those things," she'd said. "They'll grow anywhere. Thick as weeds."

"You be in charge of Charles tonight, OK?" she said now, bunching the iris stems so they stood straight up in their cut-glass vase. "Keep him out of mischief." She carried them out to the dining room where the table was hidden under droopy lace. Then she bustled back and forth between the American refrigerator, out in the front hall beside the coats, and the Swedish refrigerator, the size of a small safe in the corner of the kitchen. She was a tall woman, and a case of complicated pneumonia during the winter had stolen from her body not only its flesh but also its disciplined competence. "What am I looking for? What am I doing?" she kept asking herself. "How stupid can you get?" She poured a bowl of runny red Jell-O down the sink and began again. She lit the old stove. "What am I forgetting?" she muttered, checking the clock.

She was fixing foods she had served hundreds of times, which Father and we children had as often uncritically consumed—black-eyed peas and lentils, celery smeared with peanut butter, Del Monte fruit cocktail suspended in cherry Jell-O. But suddenly these were difficult, elusive. The worried V deepened between her brows. As the afternoon wore on, her eyes took on the haggard look of someone fending off ruin, the dark winter look that made me nervous.

She couldn't blame the distress on my father: it wasn't his idea to invite Dr. Ramaswami for dinner, a man known to become ill at the mention of meat, who thought eating eggs just short of murder. He had explained his views to her one afternoon at the Embassy of India, during a tea which she had attended willingly, full of curiosity about reincarnation and the winding of saris, without seams or safety pins or anything. She came home satisfied instead with news of a Hindu sect whose members never went outside for fear of inflicting pain on the grass and stones.

"Maybe that's the answer," she said to Father, who had flopped down beside me on the couch the minute he'd helped her off with her shawl, picked up a comic book, and was now out of reach.

"I'm going upstairs to change," she said, but she couldn't move because my baby brother, Georgie, had his arms around her knees. She plucked her shawl off the couch with a flourish, tucked it under one arm, then draped it over the other shoulder. "I said, maybe that's the answer, Frank."

Later she was to ravage the iris.

My father looked up and then nudged me with a wink. "What was the question?" he asked.

THEY grew along the side of the house under the window. One day there were swellings at the tips of the stems; over the course of the next, a first flower uncrimped itself; by morning it shone forth, an unbelievable glory of ruffles. I ran into the house calling her, knowing I would get no response, and knowing exactly where she was, but calling because the sight of such a flower made me want to make noise.

"You've got to see something," I panted. She lay face down on a towel on the balcony over the garage. Charles and Georgie traced her naked body with their trucks.

She swiveled her head so her words would come my way. "What is it?"

"I don't know," I said. "You'll just have to see."

"I want to see, I want to see," sang six-year-old Charles, but when he did follow us down and I put his face right up to one, he said, "Where?"

"Oh, Cynthia," she said. In the dark midst of winter she had almost died. Now she couldn't tear herself away from the sun. "There's nothing like it," she told my father with a laugh, whom the mildest light burned to a crisp. "I've got to feel it in the marrow of my bones." Father didn't think that was a good idea. "Breast cancer, or something," he said. "Besides, what will the children?"

"Please," I said. "Just for a minute."

She pushed herself up to a sitting position. Her skin in front bore the rashy imprint of the towel. She had lost such terrible weight being sick that her breasts sagged like empty pouches and you could see every knob of her spine. And the sun, while it browned her body, seemed also to have covered it with a fine grey dust.

"Get me a robe then," she said.

I did and handed it out to her. I went in front of her down the stairs carrying Georgie. Charles tagged along behind. By then the excitement had dissipated—the conviction that I had come across something she'd been looking for all winter, something that might make a difference to her.

By then, they were just bearded iris, common, weedy. But she cupped the purple head and drew it over to us. She stroked one of its three lolling tongues. "These are sort of funny, aren't they, these little hairs. Want to touch?"

I touched where she had, the dark purple tuft in its throat, too soft to feel. I peered into its folded core. It was the name that was funny—bearded iris. It made me remember a carnival in Florida—a muggy tent that smelled of something gone bad, me holding my father's hand, a woman towering on a platform above us. Her face and body were stippled with clumps of dark hair. Black hair crawled from the crotch of her bathing suit down her thighs. I hung onto my father's hand, who stared impassively. She raised her arms and tufts of black hair bloomed. She began to move her hips. My father, who'd joined the Navy to see the world, kept staring, expressionless. I think it was his blank face that challenged her, urged her on. While at home, clutching the baby Charles in her arms, sat my mother, who knew all about carnivals—they were dangerous, and sleazy, and they gypped you. I held my father's hand and considered myself very lucky to be there.

She released the flower and it bobbed upright again on its long taut stem. *Bearded iris,* I thought, and was happy because at that moment I knew it was my favorite flower, and how many girls my age had such a thing, and felt so absolutely sure?

The next morning, more iris bloomed, promises. Every day

new blossoms defied the everyday. My friend in the neighborhood, Pia Brandberg, was always teaching me to juggle, and we took particular care as we bounced our balls against the wall that belonged to the iris. When I did, by sheer accident, land a ball in their midst, I whispered apologies and tried to infuse my juggling for a while afterward with the spirit of remorse.

THE iris centerpiece was so tall I couldn't see Charles across the table. No one felt the desecration except me.

Dr. Ramaswami sat on my mother's right beside me. He was small and thin, not much taller than I was, with brown skin and pale, yellowish cheeks. His nose and chin were sharp, and his protruding eyes seemed like a woman's, half-asleep, with long lashes. He wore a light suit that shone, a rosy tie, and on his head, what I had hoped for, a silk turban. I knew Charles, sitting opposite him, would be staring shamelessly. There was nothing I could do about it but make sure my own eyes moved around the table in a natural fashion. It was enough that the turban perched there on Dr. Ramaswami's head, a bright cloud at the edge of my vision, while he sat at our table. You didn't have to behold a turban every possible second with your eyes. With Charles, enough was never enough.

The centerpiece shielded our guest from Georgie, whose high chair had been moved to my father's right across from me because he still ate with his hands.

"OK, who stole the burgers?" my father said, when we had all settled in our places.

"Burgers?" asked our guest.

My mother gave him one of her smile-edged frowns. It was to disconnect her not only from the thoughtless remark but also from my father. She had smoothed baby oil on her skin and it was a rich, dust-free brown against the white of her gypsy blouse, the bright pink of her lipstick. Her voice sounded different, studied. The afternoon's turmoil was well in check.

"You are most fortunate," Dr. Ramaswami told my father in a sweet, high voice, "that your family is here with you."

"That's a good one," Mother said.

"You're so right," said Father at the same time.

We all sipped our apple juice. It had come to her at the last minute that the human consumption of milk might violate the rights of cows. My father loved milk, said he was like a little boy where milk was concerned.

"As you do, I have also two sons," said Dr. Ramaswami, "but they must stay in Calcutta with their mother." He seemed to speak everything in the cadence of a question.

"Your wife?" asked my mother.

"I was fourteen when the marriage took place. She was thirteen."

My father whistled. My mother studied our guest's face intently, as if waiting for him to finish what he meant to say.

"Cynthia, here, will be thirteen," Father said.

Dr. Ramaswami turned his sleepy gaze on me. I gripped the sides of my chair and stared at Georgie who had a single bean stuck to his forehead like a growth. There was a terrible silence during which I felt expected to say something—to confirm or deny what everyone was thinking about me, except that I wasn't sure what that was.

"OK, where's my burger?" Charles said, to my relief, from behind the centerpiece, and I promised myself I would try to stop hating him.

"Oh Charles, for heaven's sake," said Mother, and Father chimed in with a question about our guest's "line of work."

Dr. Ramaswami had been sent to Stockholm by the government of India to study at the Institute of Meteorology. "There is a great machine, the size of this room, larger." He lifted his hands; his thin brown fingers seemed boneless; he sang, "We bring it numbers. It draws maps for us. It explains weather."

"Whether what?" my father asked, and Mother's head flinched with a groan.

"One hopes always for greater understanding, greater precision, one day, perhaps, control. In my country, you see, weather is everything—politics, economics, religion." He glanced at my mother. "Even love." Her penciled eyebrows arched at the word.

"In the hot season, wives desert husbands for the mountains. We husbands dig holes in the earth and bury ourselves, praying to survive." He stopped and smiled shyly at everyone to show he was joking. His eyes came to rest on Mother, who gazed blankly at the tablecloth, outlining one of the lace daisies with her finger. Then Dr. Ramaswami looked sidelong in the direction of my father. "In my country, even the military is nothing," he said. "Nothing when compared to the weather."

"How come we can't taste saliva?" Charles asked.

"Because we're used to it, son," my father said.

"Then could Cynthia taste my saliva and could I taste—"

"Please don't humor him," Mother said to Father. To our guest, she said, "Here you've got to bury yourself in clothes. The woolen stockings, and woolen socks, and woolen sweaters, it's hardly worth the trouble to get dressed in the morning."

Dr. Ramaswami sighed gently. "All winter I am fat with sweaters. And still I am never warm enough."

"I got so I could take the cold." Her voice dropped and she leaned close to Dr. Ramaswami, as if she'd decided not to bore the rest of us with what we already knew. "But that darkness all the time, that's what really gets to you." Her eyes seemed to retreat at the memory.

"Indeed," said Dr. Ramaswami. "Yet in my country the sun is a brutal enemy."

"You're not kidding," my father said loudly. He leaned to one side to see around the iris. "Remember, Angie, I told you about Bombay." To our guest: "We dropped anchor for a couple days off Bombay."

Mother held one thin brown arm in the air and studied it closely. "Now I practically worship the sun," she said, then watched the arm settle back onto the lace cloth beside Dr. Ramaswami's hand, as though it didn't belong to her.

"You happen to notice the skirt she's wearing?" my father called down the table. "I picked it up in the Bombay bazaar. Show him, Angie. You like that skirt?"

She pretended not to hear.

"Is that where you got us those bells with the little brass elephants?" I flushed at the sound of my own voice. Father knew I knew it was. Meanwhile Charles leaned down and grabbed the hem of Mother's blue and purple skirt and raised it above the tabletop. She yanked it from his hand and smoothed her lap.

"In my country water is the element of life. We worship rain. There is a chant in Hindi that begins *You are heaven's moisture*. It is about a goddess." Dr. Ramaswami spoke with his eyes lowered to his plate, where one hand moved a fork under the last portion of beans then inserted them into his mouth.

"That's beautiful," my mother said, passing him the pink ring mold of Jell-O and a smile as drowsy as his own.

"You give birth to the water-cleansed moon. . . ." He poked gently at the Jell-O with his fork. "You will excuse me," he said finally, handing it on to me. I peered into its translucence, thinking maybe he'd seen a fly trapped among the tiny cubes of fruit. "Certain restrictions do not permit me," he said.

"From eating Jell-O?" my mother asked, still smiling, sure this was another little joke.

Dr. Ramaswami touched the ring again. It shivered on its plate between us. "Commonly derived from animal protein," he said, and his nose pinched in reflex.

There was a moment of thick silence, ended by a shriek of recognition from Georgie: he loved red Jell-O. He thrust one fat fist toward it like a Hitler salute, opening and closing.

"No," Mother said, very calm. "No. Not Royal cherry Jell-O." She was up and disappearing into the kitchen. There were sounds like an animal scratching, rummaging. Father spooned Jell-O into Georgie's bowl.

She returned with a small torn piece of cardboard, held it before her like a sacred text, and recited, "Sugar, gelatine, artificial flavors, dimethipro-something."

Dr. Ramaswami waved one long, boneless finger from side to side. "Gelatine," he said, shaking his head.

"Frank." Mother turned to Father, her shoulders hunched forward, hugging herself as though she were all at once cold. "What's in gelatine, Frank?"

"It's all right, Angie," Father said.

"They don't make Jell-O out of animals, do they?" she pleaded. "Isn't it all just chemicals now?"

Father got up and led her back to her seat. "I'm not sure," he said. "It could be." He gave her shoulder a squeeze and the bones made a noise.

She wouldn't look at the table now but gazed off to the side at the floor between her and Dr. Ramaswami. "I thought I had it all figured out," she murmured. "I didn't think . . ."

"This is my fault," announced our guest. "I beg you to pardon—"

She straightened herself abruptly. "It's nothing," she said, like an iron gate dropping down—we knew about that. "You don't want to take any chances." She tore the Jell-O box in half, then tried to tear the two pieces in half again but hadn't the strength. "But I want you to know that in the States they do everything with chemicals now. Pretty soon we'll just take pills morning and night instead of all this foolishness about eating. I won't regret the day, I'll tell you that."

"In my country, what you speak of would be a welcome advance. Tens of thousands die everyday of starvation."

"You folks've got to learn how to handle those cows—show 'em who's boss," my father said.

"Perhaps." Dr. Ramaswami put his hand over Mother's, fisted around the crumpled Jell-O box. "I have enjoyed this evening very much."

Watching sidelong, I saw her present to Dr. Ramaswami her patient face, preoccupied, slightly condescending—the rest of us knew well that face. Then like some trick photograph, its contours went blurry. For a moment it was a face that didn't know how it wanted to look. Then it composed itself and became a face I had never seen before: brow and mouth turned smooth, softened; eyes gone wide with gratitude. A face I'd hoped someday to discover myself: it said, *yes this is what I have been waiting for yes you are what I need.*

Dr. Ramaswami did not move his hand nor did my mother move hers, whose skin was almost as dark. I looked around in panic. The bouquet of iris threw purple shadows everywhere. My father hadn't noticed. He was busy pinching up chunks of Jell-O from Georgie's tray and flicking them back in his bowl. I stood up and made a curtsey so deep I almost fell. Such gestures had been taught me during the year by the Sisters at L'Ecole Française Internationale to accompany any change in position, and I could think of nothing else to do, except maybe drop my plate. Instead I picked it up, and with another more balanced curtsey removed our guest's and stacked it on top. "Charles," I said, much louder than I intended.

"What?" he said, knowing full well.

"You're supposed to too," I said.

"Coffee?" asked my father, cheerily.

"Thank you, no," Dr. Ramaswami said, finally wiping his hands on his napkin and giving it to Charles. "Coffee is terrible for the bowels."

Charles could not suppress a snort.

"We have tea," my mother said, as if roused from sleep. She couldn't have heard him say *bowels* because what she said next was, "I think I'll show Dr. Ramaswami around the garden," and she'd never called our yard—any of our rented yards anywhere—a garden before. A garden of her own was what she'd never in fourteen years of marriage possessed—full sun, rich dark soil, improved year after year, nothing left to chance. She said a couple of rosebushes here and there weren't a garden. A stand of dauntless iris certainly wasn't.

MY father always washed the dishes. He said it helped him keep his nails and cuticles soft, which made them less interesting to his teeth. He liked to sit Mother down on the living-room sofa after supper and put a book in her lap, as if that were not the precise way she spent hours of every day. He liked to play Twenty Questions with Charles and me, and this night it was Charles's turn to think of something, my turn to ask human, male, living? Then I didn't want to guess anymore. I knew before we started he would pick Dr. Ramaswami because Dr. Ramaswami had said *bowels*. Father asked *athlete* and *movie star,* and whether he was on American TV, for which Charles pined like paradise lost.

I didn't want to reach the answer, I was so tired of our guest. I'd had enough of his weird country and I didn't care if I never saw him again, except that I longed to run from window to window, and peer into the steady twilight, and discern them—him and my mother—her, tall and very thin, him small and thin as a boy. He had touched her hand. He had changed her face.

Every now and then I heard voices, light laughter, the chime of elephant bells. What was there to show him in the yard? One gawky flowering bush, some wild blue cornflowers, a few lily buds among the shambles of the back fence. It was no garden, where only the fittest survived.

My iris. All at once I knew they were on the side of the house under my bedroom window disturbing my iris. They were poking open the ruffled petals, prodding disrespectful fingers into each core, crushing the little tufts of intangible hair. They were doing all this, and my father didn't care, he couldn't even guess it in twenty turns. He didn't even notice I wasn't playing because I already knew, and because I thought maybe if we didn't guess the answer, it wouldn't be happening, even though I hoped that it would have to be happening, even though I couldn't want it to and wouldn't guess. It reminded me of the winter before, the afternoon we lost Charles—I didn't really want him to be frozen dead under a mound of snow, yet I sensed such disaster would confer some distinction on me which I could get no other way.

"Dr. Ramaswami!" Charles shouted finally, tickled to have stumped our father, who never did go easy on him.

As if announced, a moment later we heard Mother's voice in the front hall praising the long summer sunsets of the north, and then that other voice, laid over hers, half incredulous, half bemused, like an alien chant none of us would ever learn.

Everyone Catch
on Love

*J*AG *tale lille Svenska* — Pia Brandberg, whose English was flawless, taught me to say those words to ward off everyone in the village but her. I spoke little Swedish because I was struggling to memorize much French for the Sisters at L'Ecole Française. Each dark winter morning, I rode the train into Stockholm, squeezed among grown-ups in long, gray coats. In my lap was *Une jolie maison à la campagne,* open to one more chapter in the lives of the family Lebrun. The father, a doctor, worked in the hospital and carried a valise. When the mother was not *au marché,* she could be found in the house happily knitting or serving soup. Maurice and Jeanne were model children: *gentils et intelligents.* In the month of August they enjoyed a trip to the seashore; in autumn, they wisely remembered umbrellas.

My own father was a naval officer assigned to the embassy, and the house we rented outside Stockholm you would never have called *jolie,* its pale stucco flaking off like dead skin, its green shutters askew. My younger brother Charles was already nothing but trouble, Georgie still wallowed in being the baby, and my mother had grown so unhappy by midwinter that she almost died. As for myself, I had discovered the comforts of stupidity—the blank gaze, the shrug, the silly smile. I actually spoke little anything on my own initiative. Speech in whatever language had come to feel like recitation, like one more irrelevant story, or a dangerous dream.

But Pia Brandberg, shunned by other girls in the village, had chosen me as her disciple, and when it was finally summer, and our free days endless, she led me down to Lake Malaren where we claimed a giant spruce as our fort. Under the dark dome of its lowest drooping branches, we constructed furniture from stones, pieces of bark, luckily shaped twigs, a found board. The floor, spongy with fallen needles, gave under us, and the still air was redolent of mushrooms. Somedays we ventured out to forage for wild blueberries—Pia tested them first, and then we waited to see if she would die.

Once as we picked our way along the shore, Pia pointed to a dark brown bottle wedged by the current between two rocks, an interesting bottle, short of neck and round. "We shall make use of that," she said, already sunk to the ground, one foot in her hands, dragging off the shoe without untying it. "I shall do it," she added, as she always did, when I made motions to follow.

"Maybe there's something inside. A letter." I offered this as incentive, for I was just as content to watch her inch her way out into the icy water, lose her footing on the uneven bottom, stagger up, continue on, reach. Her narrow feet were blue when she clambered back up the shore and her pants soaked past the knees. She twisted off the rusty cap, inverted the bottle, and shook it, but only a little water dripped out. "Look inside," I said. "Maybe there's a message." I was liking that idea.

She turned her back to the sun, squinted one eye, then her face twisted as if in pain. She thrust the bottle under my nose. "Let me out of here," I screamed and scrambled away up the rocks.

Pia looked up at me, her thin lips curving between a smirk and a frown. Maybe she was considering a game of chasing me with the bottle, and its nasty smell for which we shared no name. She said nothing.

"Throw it away," I said.

She turned and reentered the water; she held the bottle under until it was full then lifted it high and poured the water out.

"Come on, Pia, throw it away," I said.

She dipped and poured. She wouldn't take her eyes off her hand; her pointed chin was set.

Her frozen legs almost buckled under her when she tried to climb out. I offered a hand. She made a feint with the bottle and I shrank back. Then without picking up her shoes and socks, she started back to our tree, her bare feet numb to pricks and stubs. She walked right into a clump of thistles and bent off the tallest stalk. She gathered plumes of wild grass. After she arranged these stems in the bottle, she propped it against the central trunk. It made everything else in our fort seem pretend.

PIA told me that when the girls in the village moved from Folk-school to the Gymnasium they acquired numbers, according to how far they would go. For purposes of the system, the female body was divided at the waist. And first the top half, then the bottom must yield progressively to touching outside the clothes, touching inside the clothes, then viewing naked. The final seventh stage was something Pia called *fornication,* a word I understood immediately to mean that impossibly embarrassing act my mother had tried to describe for me a lifetime ago and never mentioned since.

One day after lunch, I was sitting on the cement steps at the foot of our front yard waiting for Pia. We were going down to the square to buy a hank of licorice with pooled coins, then on to the tree fort. From the other end of the lane two girls strolled in my direction. Last year, when my family had just moved into the neighborhood, I had spent whole Saturdays watching girls like these glide giggling past our house. If only I could get rid of Pia, I used to think, if only she would stay away for one hour, I was sure these other pretty girls would stop and ask my name, invite me to go with them, share the secret of their hilarity and poise.

Now two of those better and long-awaited girls were bending

their path from the center of the road toward the place where I sat. My easy heart began to drum.

The tall one, Annika, had a way of flaring her nostrils and tossing her long red-blond hair like an impatient horse. Eva was smaller, rounder, with blond feathery waves and freckles. She hugged herself when she laughed. They were wearing identical sleeveless summer dresses printed with bouquets of flowers, white ankle socks and wide flat sandals. The leather of Annika's was riddled with tiny holes. Both mouths were pale orange and their nails matched. With a dark pencil, they had both added long upturned hooks to the outer edges of their eyes.

Soon I could hardly breathe. Thanks to Pia, I knew more than I wanted to know about Annika, who was stopping in front of me, tossing her hair and asking, "Will you walk?" Her low voice seemed to turn that simple question to a challenge.

"I am waiting for Pia Brandberg," I said.

"Ah," said Annika on an indrawn breath, throwing Eva a look. "Ah," said Eva, suppressing a giggle. She stepped back into the road so she could survey its length. "I no see her," she said.

At first I thought the clumsy negative was a joke, I was so used to Pia's perfect English, but neither girl seemed to react to the error. Briefly it freed me from my own sense of inferiority—long enough for me to stand up and go along.

In less than a minute, I knew I'd made a mistake. They continued to talk to each other in Swedish, and though I was taller than Eva, I felt like a mindless baby who must be careful not to wander off and get lost. I moved each foot deliberately trying to keep to their slow pace. Now and then we stepped aside and stopped while a car passed.

Nous nous promenons, I told myself, and my mind took up the conjugation of that reflexive verb, one past tense after another. There came a silence. They seemed to expect me to say something. *The blossoming apple tree resembles a fresh bouquet,* I might have exclaimed. *The wheat undulates gently in the adjoining fields.* Such were the observations of Jeanne Lebrun when she made a *promenade* in spring, but there were no wheatfields or apple trees in sight. I told them their dresses were pretty. Annika said, "We make them in sewing class." Eva pulled from her pocket a round tin of blue candies. Like Annika, I pinched one up and placed it on my tongue. It was intensely peppermint. We breathed in and out with open mouths, savoring the cool sting. I looked back as we turned the corner at the foot of the final hill. I was expecting Pia, her wiry, no-nonsense, sometimes furious walk. *I no see her.*

In twice the time it would have taken Pia and me, we arrived at the square: the train platform, an ice-cream kiosk, and on either side of the tracks, shops with orange and green awnings. Annika and Eva exchanged more sentences in Swedish, finally agreeing that our first stop should be the shop called Ingrid's, with its molded brassieres and lace petticoats, its bin of bright pink lipstick bullets in plastic cases, its collection of screw-back earrings. After that we hung around the stationer's, riffling slowly through fashion magazines, pointing out glamorous hairdos and dresses, acknowledging each with a quick intake of breath. Then came a contemptuous search through the general clothing store for something "new style," then a tour of dry goods, caressing chintz florals, fingering ribbons, lace trims, gold and silver buttons.

I tried through it all to harmonize my noises and gestures with theirs: where they worshiped, I worshiped; where they disapproved, so did I. After a while, I began to feel sleepy. I began to crave that licorice, and maybe an ice-cream bar, a cinnamon bun from the Konditori. I couldn't understand why Annika and Eva were not interested in important, edible things. In between shops, they stopped and checked their reflections in the windows and if necessary combed hair. I stared off down the open field that stretched in the distance to the lake's shore. I wondered where Pia was. Somewhere among the rocks rising into hills on my right was our tree. Maybe it was the one I could see pushing above the others into the blue, remotely clouded sky.

Before starting home, we stood for some time on the train platform studying a film poster. It was a distant, badly focused, black-and-white photograph of a man and a woman. They seemed to be running through a forest, the woman in the lead. They weren't wearing any clothes. If you looked away from the picture, you caught in the corner of your eye, emerging from the blur, the contour of the woman's nipple, the shadow of hair below the waist. The man's body was concealed below the chest by hers. I had noticed the poster before, it and others similarly revealing; noticed, then pretended not to. This was Sweden; the Swedes had no *false modesty,* my mother liked to declare, as she sunbathed on the garage roof stripped to bare skin. Still I had never dared stare openly at such pictures the way Eva was now. She shifted from one sandal to the other, she chewed her cheek. Annika was tossing her mane. "*På cinema,*" she said to me indifferently. I nodded. At the bottom of the poster were the words that described many Swedish movies — *barn verbjudet. Children forbidden* — it seemed for that moment like a taunt, scornful and unfair.

Eva looked up at me, her eyes wide. "Ooh la la," she said, without conviction.

"What does that say?" I asked, pointing to another strip of words, as though the name of the movie were all that interested me.

The two conferred again in Swedish and seemed finally to disagree. "*A Jolly Summer,*" Annika said, while Eva shook her head.

We began to climb the hill to our neighborhood. The trees lining the road closed over us. I kept walking ahead, then having to stop and wait for the two of them to catch up. I wanted to think in some systematic way about that forbidden movie, what it might show, but I found myself distracted by French phrases, vestiges of Maurice and Jeanne's expedition to the cinema to see a film about *Tarzane,* a young man and strong, who jumped from branch to branch. He spoke to the elephants, the monkeys were his friends. But, the story cautioned, there were fierce lions, serpents, crocodiles: that was the easy part, for the words were the same in English and French.

Each time I stopped and turned around, I saw Eva nudge Annika. Finally I went ahead again, figuring to wave a nonchalant good-bye at Pia's corner and be gone, when Annika's long fingers stretched from nowhere, gripped my arm and dragged me back between them. She gave two delicate coughs.

"Do you," she said, then paused. "Will you . . ." She looked at Eva and asked, "Love?" Eva didn't know, so she drew a breath and finished: "Will you love Oskar Lindstrom?"

The verb and then the name at the end seemed to jar a funny bone that ran through my whole body.

I started to shrug humbly, but Annika shook my arm. "Will you love Oskar Lindstrom?" She was certain now she had the words right.

"Me?" I asked stupidly, hoping to convey the absurdity of the question.

Eva poked me on the other side. "Will you kiss Oskar Lindstrom?" Her eyes laughed.

"Me?" I lurched out of Annika's grip and darted some quick steps ahead of them.

"Oskar sayze he loves you," sang Eva.

I was walking up the hill backward, denying her song. But I couldn't turn and run away. I wanted to hear their questions again, and again. Often enough that I could answer them. I couldn't remember whether kisses were on Pia's sexual ladder. If so, where were they, at the bottom? The Lebrun children had never had occasion to kiss anyone except their grandparents, but once in the courtyard at L'Ecole Française, the only boy in our class, François, had trapped me—"*Baises-moi*," he'd insisted, gagging me with the odor of infected sinuses. Once you stepped onto the kissing rung, was the climb ineluctable? Then I remembered what I had been trying all afternoon not to think about: Annika was a seven. How could she be? How could she have taken all the clothes off that tall, proud body, swaying up the hill? Opened her legs? How could she act now as though nothing had happened?

"Oskar is very nice boy," Annika said, teasing. Then her voice turned grim, almost sad. "Very nice boy," she said.

"Not boy," said Eva. "*Teen-aicher.*"

OSKAR Lindstrom was the only child of Fru Lindstrom, one of the handful of women who had been through enough suffering to become my mother's friend. Fru Lindstrom communicated with my mother in a mixture of Swedish, English, and pure emotion, coded in contortions of the body and face. Occasionally she slipped into unpopular German, her native tongue, but after anything more than a word or phrase, her voice trailed off in shame. When they conversed in our kitchen, sipping tea and nibbling ginger wafers, my mother tended to look off to one side and allow silences, half-skeptical yet half-enamored of Fru Lindstrom's tireless optimism and vitality, for those things had always eluded her. Fru Lindstrom's desire to reassure was so intense that her smiles became painful grimaces. When she laughed, her eyes streamed with tears.

When my mother caught pneumonia, Fru Lindstrom visited every other day, kept filled a vase by her bed with fresh flowers from Holland. I wished she would bring food, because my father was no cook, and it was cereal, tomato soup, and peanut butter for supper every night—a far cry from dinner *chez la famille Lebrun:* a table set in good taste, platters of meat and green beans, Marguerite, *la domestique,* who carried them away to the kitchen when empty and brought in the dessert, that is to say, the cheese and the fruits. When my mother's birthday came, my father and I tried to bake a cake to surprise her, but somehow he thought I put in the cup of sugar and I thought he did, and the cake came out flat as a plate, tasteless and hard.

Fru Lindstrom, I learned later, was no cook either, nor did she believe in large meals—"a little of dis und dat"—a cracker with sour cream, a boiled potato, smoked herring from the village market, some fraction of a kilo. Her husband, whose business, Lindstrom Instruments, did rather well, she left to his own devices. He preferred to eat in town. We saw him now and then on weekends, working on his old black Mercedes.

All along I had been only dimly conscious of Oskar. In the winter, he might pass me on his bike, a sack of books strapped to his back and on his head a man's woollen cap. Now that the weather was warm, I caught glimpses of him shirtless on the running board of his father's car, stretching to polish the roof. On still afternoons I might hear the slippery chords of his harmonica as somewhere he prowled the scale looking for jazz.

But nothing snagged. He was just there, long and raw-boned, oblivious, undistinguished except for a lower lip that drooped and heavy, dark eyebrows that met in confusion on the bridge of his nose.

The only time I had spoken to him was during the swimming trip our mothers planned to Angby Beach when summer began, for which Fru Lindstrom asked Oskar to be the chauffeur. She sat up front in the Mercedes, her head tipped onto his shoulder, and playfully scolded him the whole way for driving too fast. I sat in the back with my mother and the boys, breathing deep the leather upholstery, trying to remember what the smell reminded me of, and pretending Charles didn't exist. Over and over, he whined, "When are we going to go swimming, you said we were going swimming." Of course when we got there, and Mother snapped his shirt up over his head, he just stood and rubbed his inner arms against his bare sides. Fru Lindstrom gave him a push between the shoulder blades in the direction of the water, and he ducked sideways out of reach. He spent the rest of the afternoon sitting hunched under a towel on a corner of the blanket, counting things.

We all had on bathing suits underneath, but I was still embarrassed to be unbuttoning my shirt, sliding my shorts down over my hips. I folded my discarded clothes so that the inside of each garment, the part that bore the touch and smell of my body, was out of sight. I stayed crouched on the blanket: what now? When the family Lebrun spent a day by the edge of the sea, the sky was never so blue nor the sun so brilliant, and they each knew what to do. The mother, having filled a basket with plums, went back to knitting happily in the shadow of a parasol. Doctor Lebrun fished. Maurice and Jeanne bathed in the tepid water. In the last paragraph, Jeanne dug a large hole in the sand in which she found a shell. The outside was rough and gray, the inside, pink and smooth. Jeanne slid her finger into the opening. Something soft rested in the depths. Happily, she ran to show her mother. The dry sand crunched under her steps.

I stole a look up at Oskar. He was just standing there unashamed in baggy knitted briefs, his hands in his armpits, staring sternly at the water.

Fru Lindstrom had stripped all Georgie's clothes off, patted him on his bare bottom, and said, "So, you are Swedish now." In the shallow water closest to us, contained by bullety floats, children paddled without bathing suits or sat naked digging in the sand. Georgie grabbed himself and froze to his spot.

"Do you have to go to the bathroom," my mother whispered loudly. He didn't move. She gently removed his hands. "Where's his leash?" She rummaged through her straw bag, extracted it length by length.

"Oh no, no, no," Fru Lindstrom cried, cupping both hands over one breast. "He moost *spielen*. Play." She lifted Georgie and swung him around. "Play, play, play."

My mother won. The leash was for Georgie's own good. She folded over the waist of her bathing suit bottom until her navel showed like Fru Lindstrom's. "He can still play," she said. "I hold one end, so he won't wander off and drown." She emphasized each verb with a different motion of the hands. She and Fru Lindstrom were stretching out side by side in the center of the blanket, undoing the straps of their tops. They were both brown as bottles, though my mother's skin puckered everywhere from being sick. Again she shook Georgie's fists away from his crotch, then she wrapped her end of the leash an extra time around her hand, her head dropped to the blanket, her eyes closed, and she gave in to the spell of the sun.

I was still hovering beside my outer clothes, staring resolutely at the sand, recalling too late how Maurice and Jeanne thought to bring a kite to the beach, how the breeze lifted it high in the air. Around us in full view, men and women, boys and girls were changing out of wet suits under the haphazard cover of only a towel or robe. I didn't want to see anything. I certainly didn't feel like digging a large hole. Then Oskar Lindstrom's feet stepped practically into my gaze. They were grotesquely large, with a fringe of dark hair around each ankle. I stood up in the chilly air and ran blindly for the water, splashed through the shallows, flopped finally under its cover. Fed by arctic streams, its cold was crushing, left me gasping for breath.

The water churned behind me, nearer, and then past where I sculled slowly, trying to calm my body, back and forth. It was Oskar's thrashing stroke. I noticed with satisfaction that he was breathing incorrectly, his head lurching to right and left, the front lock of his hair slapping from side to side.

Some meters beyond me, he stopped and bobbed, grinning his loose-lipped grin. "Come," he called, breathless. "It is not deep."

"Whose afraid of deep water?" I pushed off from the silky bottom and did the smooth and proper Australian crawl I'd learned when we lived in Florida, until my face ached with the cold. Oskar was now many meters away, between me and the shore, bobbing and grinning gallantly. We treaded water, both working to hide the hardship it was to draw breath.

"Here it is deep," Oskar gasped.

"How deep?" I asked indifferently.

He pointed to the sky, his head lifted a few inches above the surface, then sank; the water slid up his raised arm to the wrist, and then even the tip of his finger was gone. Everything was quiet. The shrieks of the naked children near shore blended into distant irrelevance, like background birds. Finally his head broke the surface. He whipped his hair back from his face. His mouth still gaped cheerfully, but his eyes looked pink and surprised. "I don't find it," he said. "No floor."

All at once I saw Oskar and me from far away, two tiny wiggling creatures suspended above a giant chasm, and all that black water only an illusion of support. At any minute we could be dragged down into the gorge, toward the further mouth, where even colder currents had their source.

Very calmly, I began crawling for shore. Palms cupped, bent elbows lifted high, six fluttering kicks to each stroke.

I LAY in my room off the kitchen sleepless, not this time because I was afraid of the dark but because there was no dark now that it was summer, only a fluorescent, humming twilight. My parents had driven into the city to eat dinner; afterward they would go to the cinema, a new film, recommended by Fru Lindstrom: "very fine, very beautiful." It was their anniversary. According to Fru Lindstrom the movie was called *One Summer of Happiness.*

"But it's in Swedish," my father said that afternoon. "I won't get a single word."

"You'll catch on," my mother said, patting his upper arm.

"Everyone catch on love," said Fru Lindstrom. Less and less often was she bothering to efface herself when my father was home. Instead she seemed to be teaching my mother how to humor him, how to lavish attention on him, yet ignore him all the while.

"Fourteen years of marriage," Fru Lindstrom said, touching her tongue to her upper lip, cocking her head. "You were some handsome *poiken, nicht wahr?*"

My father shook his head. "I was the skinniest, pimpliest, dumbest klutz. . . ."

Fru Lindstrom looked puzzled.

"She'll tell you," he said.

"I was very young," my mother said. "He was a college boy."

Now half-awake, I went over the story, readied the place for my parents first to meet—mid-June, a village in the Poconos, the shop that sold homemade ice cream. Inside, my mother sat at a round marble table and wiped chocolate from the blank face of the child she was taking care of. A fan turned overhead. Outside the window, my father stared at her through his reflection; his family had summered in the village for years and she was a stranger. The double doors were open. The sky had been never so blue, nor the sun so brilliant. In he walked.

In my mind they always kissed soon after his entrance, I pronounced them man and wife, and myself immaculately born. And we were happy then, the three of us—I would have liked to tell Fru Lindstrom that, but I couldn't remember exactly when it was, or where.

Fourteen years later, I decided, it was Charles and Georgie who had more or less worn my mother out. They were in bed now, and I was supposed to make sure they stayed there. My mother was happy tonight, happier that she had been since long before she'd stood at death's door. I'd watched her and Father's backs seem to sink into the front yard as they went down the cement steps to the road. She was wearing the full, bright skirt from Bombay, a shawl from Spain. She held his arm and her hips swayed. They were going to see a movie in Swedish about love—*One Summer of Happiness.* All at once, with a shock, I realized something. That was the same film I'd seen on the poster, the naked man and woman, the one Annika called *A Jolly Summer.* I was jerked wide awake with indignation. They should not be going to see such things. *You'll catch on,* my mother said, holding Father's arm, swaying her hips. *Watch out,* I wanted to warn him. *Watch out.*

THERE was a pale spot of light on the ceiling of my room. I was still not asleep, and the spot twitched across the plaster, brightening, and began to slide down the wall next to my bed. I opened my mouth to scream and the spot disappeared.

Blood throbbed in my ears. The spot was on the ceiling again, pale and wide. This time I noticed the translucent ribbon tying it to my open window, and worse, to something else outside, a burglar, the crazed murderer I had been expecting from the moment I was assigned this bedroom by myself, downstairs. Trembling, I slipped out of bed and crept up to Charles and Georgie's room; they were sleeping noisily. With my head pressed to their window frame, I inched one eye around. And there in the purplish shadows of the side yard was Oskar Lindstrom, squatting in the grass, sighting down the flashlight in his hand as though it were a gun.

Naturally I was relieved that it was only he, but then I resented having been scared. It seemed to me that Oscar Lindstrom had intruded into my life one too many times. Aroused in the cause of justice, I ran down to the kitchen, dug through a drawer of used candles and first-aid cream for our flashlight. Then I raced back to the boys' window, took a long breath, stuck my flashlight around the frame and flicked it on. If it had been a brush, I'd have painted circles around Oskar Lindstrom. By the time he thought to lift his shaggy brow, I'd flicked it off.

I leaned against the wall panting. In a minute the faintest spot shone on the ceiling, waving slightly from side to side, accompanied by the tinny chords of a harmonica.

I tiptoed back to my room, prepared to take my chances,

stepped right into the window, and blasted him in the face with my beam. Then I ducked.

His light leaped to my ceiling, flickered on and off, on and off. I didn't breathe.

"Come out tonight," I heard him call. "It is not dark."

Did he think I was afraid of the dark? I rose into the window. He was standing a little below me in an open shirt, shorts, and bare feet. He kept making a hissing sound.

"Come out," he said. His face was in shadow. As a matter of pride, I shot it again with my light. Then I skipped up the stairs to wake Charles.

"Did you catch them?" Charles asked as he stirred and stretched.

"Want to go outside?" I said. He peered over the edge of his bed at the floor, then back to me with wide eyes. "No lions, no serpents, no crocodiles," I assured him as I sat him up in his underwear.

"Bugs," he murmured, putting his feet on the floor reluctantly.

I led him downstairs where I pulled on shorts and tucked in my nightgown. Raising a finger for silence, I let us out the front door.

Charles crept behind me around to the side yard, but when we saw Oskar sitting under my window, strafing it with his light, Charles called right out to him, so I had to drag him back behind the front stoop and clamp my hand over his mouth. We waited for Oskar to scout past us around to the other side, then we followed him at a distance, and just before he turned the corner into the backyard, with a surge of terror, I flashed my light at him then tore off in the other direction. Oskar and I chased like this, keeping the house between us, until I was out of breath from the suspense, the surprise, the indignation. As I ran, I was a streak of heat; when I lay still, hiding, I remembered the safety of my bed inside and shivered in the cold dew.

The trouble was Charles never got the idea and kept approaching Oskar or me openly, chattering about the bugs in his dreams. The game sort of changed into escaping from Charles instead of each other. Then it broke down. I came racing around the back of the house into the side yard where it had all started and Oskar was standing in my path, holding the glaring flashlight to his chest the way a corpse is supposed to hold flowers, but tipped to his face, so he looked like a fiend. Then he turned it off and after a minute or so my eyes adjusted to his true face—there was that droopy, innocent smile.

"Come on," he said, taking a few steps toward me, and I could smell his hair and sweat. He opened his arms.

Charles bolted from nowhere into them. "I win," he crowed.

THE tent had been in Oskar's backyard all summer, pitched in a corner beside the stand of hemlocks his lot shared with ours. I began to watch it closely—from the kitchen window, from the balcony where mother lay naked, from the shrubbery along the back of the house. I knew when Oskar was in it. I took note of the food he carried out for himself on a tray—iced buns, bread and meat, red juice; of the magazines wedged under his arm, the clothes he wore; as though these things might carry a message to me, a promise or warning, a summons. Since the night I went out to him, we had not crossed paths again. Did he no longer love me? A love born so mysteriously out of nothing might just as gratuitously die. Suppose Annika had reported the truth—No, Cynthia doesn't love you, Oskar Lindstrom? Suppose he had believed her, given up?

Sometimes I thought I heard the anguished whine of a harmonica. Or was it the sound of my own ears straining?

Every day Pia came by for me on her way to our fort.

"I don't feel well," I said. I found the silliness of our old inventions to be an insult. What was wrong with Pia that she didn't see that?

"After we walk, you will feel better," said Pia.

"I'm watching Charles and Georgie."

"You can go," came my mother's voice. "I don't need you."

But I couldn't go. I had to watch the tent. Oskar was inside, who had said he loved me. I would wander among my lookouts forever, until I discovered what that meant.

At night in bed I waited for the shaft of his light. One flash would have pulled me outside to him. I wouldn't hesitate. *Oh Oskar, Oskar,* I prayed. *One flash.*

I made up my own stories: I was juggling skillfully, as Pia had taught me, with three balls. One of them fell and rolled under the flap of the tent. Impulsively I went after it. Inside Oskar was kneeling with open arms. I took great care imagining how I looked, what I wore. Often I wound up borrowing Annika's blue flowered dress and sandals and painted dark hooks at my eyes. Oskar always looked the way he had by twilight, in baggy shorts and bare feet, fearless and half-mocking, yet for some reason, calling for me. Once I was inside the tent, the stories stalled, dissolved into the vague nakedness of a film poster, a remembered smell, a slow harmonica.

THERE was a gap in the rotting fence between our yards, where my mother and Fru Lindstrom passed through. One day I found myself standing in that gap, under a blue sky, a bright sun, dizzy with my own pulse. My blood knew: this was the moment I'd been waiting for. Oskar was in his tent; Charles, whom my mother had sent me out to fetch, was nowhere in sight. There was no reason not to walk over to the open flap, stoop down and ask, "Is my brother in here?"

It was dim inside except for the yellow light of a lantern hanging from the pole beside Oskar's head. And there he was, wearing only shorts, stretched out on an air mattress, propped on one elbow, a magazine open in front of him. He had the tiniest, flat nipples. He looked at me as though he didn't recognize who I was.

"He's supposed to come home for lunch," I said, dodging his eyes. My own were frantically taking in the sparse details—as though some answer lay in their combination.

Oskar stretched an arm at me. There was a pack of gum in his hand. I didn't move. "Have a piece," he said.

"It's almost lunch time," I said.

He flicked it onto the canvas between us with his thumb. "You can have it later."

"What are you reading?" I'd crawled inside a ways, to retrieve his offering. A humid odor clogged my throat. There was really nothing in the tent—a stack of magazines, a crust of bread and the pit of some fruit on the tray.

He showed me a full-page, intricate diagram, black and white with certain red lines. "Would you care for one?" he asked, spreading half a dozen magazines into a fan.

I could see they were all about machinery, but I wanted to stay with him, so I chose. He dragged a cushion from behind his back and pushed it at me. I sat cross-legged in my corner, the magazine on one knee, the cushion on the other, and waited for the next thing to happen. The effort to keep my breathing quiet made me feel faint. My mind strove in vain to recall its stories; instead there were numbers, one to seven, stages of submission. Children forbidden. Oskar went back to his magazine.

After he had turned many pages, he looked up at me sidelong. "Will you read?" he asked. He seemed annoyed. I nodded, tucked the cushion against my chest, spread the magazine open across both knees, and dutifully studied the pictures of disembodied hands tinkering with unrecognizable parts to unrecognizable things, captions I couldn't understand. The next page was the same. But Oskar wanted me to read; I made my eyes absorb it from top to bottom, never raising them at the scrubbing sounds of his weight shifting on the air mattress, the clink of coins or keys, the coughs. On the next page, some machine had been blown apart, its little springs and cylinders scattered neatly and labeled with numbers.

The occasional picture of something I recognized—a motorcycle or car—was not enough to keep my curiosity from sliding to the near mass of his body, its attitude. I knew he was sprawled on his back now, with something under his head that propped it at an abrupt angle. One knee was bent up, the magazine resting against its thigh. The other was turned out, pointed in my direction. There was the sound again of jingled keys in a pocket, a hissing whistle. There was my reflex—a glance in his direction. And then the hot, silent certainty of wrong.

My eyes blinked back to the magazine, the unreal diagrams, the bodiless hands. Breathing was impossible. I would not be tricked again into looking at what he'd done with his shorts. I forced my eyes down the turning pages in front of me; to myself I whispered anything I could remember about the family Lebrun. There was the time Jeanne got sick and her heart beat very quickly and her face grew pale with sadness. There was the time she climbed *la tour Eiffel* with Papa, the doctor, and had vertigo on the third stage. She was dizzy, but she saw all of Paris, the streets, the gardens, the shops. Her pleasure was extreme.

Oskar began to make the kissing noises humans use to coax animals. I refused to hear. I refused to look up again. Yet I couldn't leave, no matter how much of his body he revealed. How could I be sure this was not what I was waiting for? Just when I might have turned away and crawled home, I heard murmurs of a mountain holiday—the Doctor, Maman, Maurice and Jeanne forging up pine-covered slopes behind their guide, hardy and sure. They visited picturesque hamlets, they collected exquisite mushrooms, they emitted cries of joy. At day's end they camped beside a river and a storm arose, but they slept without fear. And all the night the rain sang sweetly on the roofs of their tents.

The Sandstone Prize in Short Fiction

1998
Dating Miss Universe: Nine Stories
Steven Polansky

1997
Radiance: Ten Stories
John J. Clayton